MY BIG SISTER IS SO BOSSY
SHE SAYS YOU CAN'T READ THIS BOOK

·······································

Mary Hershey

My big sister is so bossy

she says you can't read this book

WENDY
LAMB
BOOKS

Published by
Wendy Lamb Books
an imprint of
Random House Children's Books
a division of Random House, Inc.
New York

Visit us on the Web! www.randomhouse.com/kids
Educators and librarians, for a variety of teaching tools, visit us at
www.randomhouse.com/teachers

Library of Congress Cataloging-in-Publication Data

Hershey, Mary.
My big sister is so bossy she says you can't read this book / Mary Hershey.
p.   cm.
Summary: Ten-year-old Effie is dealing with a lot of problems, including some missing
money, losing her best friend, the death of her grandfather and more, and her mean
older sister Maxey is making things even worse.
ISBN 0-385-74681-4 (trade)—ISBN 0-385-90917-9 (library binding)   [1. Sisters—
Fiction.   2. Honesty—Fiction.   3. Schools—Fiction.   4. Grief—Fiction.
5. Friendship—Fiction.]   I. Title.
PZ7.H432428My 2005
[Fic]—dc22
2004015144

The text of this book is set in 12-point Italian Garamond.
Book design by Trish P. Watts
Printed in the United States of America
May 2005
10 9 8 7 6 5 4 3 2 1
BVG

To my parents,
who lit my faith,
and to my sister and brothers,
who kept me in stitches

······································

ACKNOWLEDGMENTS

I am profoundly grateful to my writing
fairy godmother, Lee Wardlaw,
and to the extraordinary authors
who light my path—
Robin, Ellen, Hope, Judy,
Mary, Lisa, Marni, and Val.

....

Chapter 1

Read this book at your own risk. My big sister, Maxine Colleen Maloney, said that if this pack of lies ever got published, she'd get my birthday officially canceled. And make me regret that I was ever born.

So I guess I'm going to be ten for a long time. And if you get caught reading this, she just might come after you. Maxey says she has everyone's address. (And she means *everyone*.) But this isn't any pack of lies. Lies are what caused this whole mess, and I swore when it was all over, I'd never lie again. Not even to be polite. Not even under torture.

• • •

It looked like a regular Friday morning at my house where I live in Tyler Wash, Texas. Which is famous for hail the size of snow cones and the winningest girls' basketball team. But it wasn't just any old day. It was the day that my fourth-grade class was picking our Discovery Project partners for St. Dominic's annual Science Olympics. It was a decision that could make or break your whole year.

"Stop *staring* at me, you little freak!" Maxey yelled in our bedroom, wrapping her arms around her bony white shoulders.

"I wasn't staring," I lied. She'd been bragging to her best friend, Philomena Finch, that her breasts had doubled in size in just a week. Naturally, I was curious. Far as I could tell, all she was growing was a big fat story about them.

Maxey glared daggers and pulled on an old undershirt. Ever since she turned twelve, she'd been very sensitive about me looking at her. Like all of a sudden her body is rated R, and I'm too young to see it.

Mom came to the door armed with her blow-dryer, curling iron, and the Look. It's the look she wears at the high school where she's coach. When she eyeballs you like that, it means you're about to get benched. Her players weren't the regional champions by accident. She worked them hard, but it paid off.

"Listen up, you two! If I hear any—*more*—yelling from this room today, you'll both be cleaning the garage tonight— do you hear me? Maxey, you got that? Effie?"

"Yes, ma'am," we said with two big sighs, and got busy making our beds. There was never any use arguing with Mom first thing in the morning. She woke up as Coach Maloney and didn't tolerate any funny business. She would usually turn back into a sorta nice mother after work. If she wasn't too tired from yelling and blowing her whistle all day.

I gave my comforter a final tug and set my pillow over the torn spot so Mom wouldn't see. It was just a worn-out tear, not an accident tear. Maxey had one, too, and I told her we weren't to tell Mom about it because we couldn't afford new comforters, so don't even ask. If we could get new ones, we would definitely not get any with bunnies on them like the ones we had now.

Our whole room was pretty much Bunnyville USA. Mom decorated it back when we were little girls and we had a dad living with us and we had money. There were bunnies hopping all over our beds, even the pillows—and bunny wallpaper, bunnies riding bicycles across our closet doors, bunny throw rugs, and a very scary bunny night-light that made big giant ears and whiskers on our ceiling in the dark. Maxey used to tell me that shadow was really the devil.

I sat down and tried to comb the curly knots out of my hair before Mom got her hands on it. She was about ready to cut it all off, but I promised her I'd take good care of it. I inherited a head full of wild red hair from my mom, and Maxey got stick-straight white hair with matching white eyebrows. We don't know where she got it. (For the record, Maxey is very pretty, but you didn't hear that from me.)

My sister went over to her secret stash in the closet that she didn't think I knew about. I stood up and walked over to the mirror across the room so I could spy on her better. This is a great trick I have that Maxey hasn't ever figured out. (I have a secret stash, too, but nobody in the universe knows about it.) She pulled out some makeup, which she's not allowed to wear until ninth grade, and stuffed it into her pocket. I added this to my mental list called "Things Mom Doesn't Know (Yet!) about Maxey." So far I had seven things on my list. And number three involved a boy and some serious kissy face. When I got up to ten things, I was going to sell the list to Maxey.

. . .

An hour later, we were holed up in the bathroom. "You gotta fix it!" I screamed in my loudest whisper. "I look like a first grader."

Mom did not approve of my poofy hair this morning that I got from using Maxey's full volume shampoo before going to bed with wet hair. I thought I'd fixed it kinda nice, but when Mom saw me at breakfast, she marched me into the downstairs bathroom and attacked it with mother spit and a lot of barrettes.

Maxey pulled the bunny clips out of my hair like a mean Mr. McGregor and tossed them aside. "Ow-ow-ouch!" I said.

"Effie, do you want me to fix it or not?"

"Yes! Just not so hard, okay?" Normally, Maxey wouldn't come within two feet of me like this, except when it comes to my hair. Or anyone's hair for that matter. She's crazy for it. Besides becoming an astronaut, Maxey is planning to become a hairstylist. She thinks it will give her an edge when applying to NASA. Wearing space helmets all day gives you pretty squashed hair.

"What's that for?" I yelled when she squeezed a big

blob of toothpaste into her hand. "Hey, you're *not* putting that in my hair!"

"Oh, just hush, Effie," she said, rubbing her palms together. "Hollywood stylists use toothpaste on the stars all the time." I tried to duck, but she nailed me in a headlock. She slicked back the tops and sides of my hair, plastering it to my skull. I closed my eyes and gave up until she finished. Trying to stop Maxey was like trying to stop an earthquake, my grandpa always said, up until he died. "Sometimes, kid," he said, "it's better to just hang on and wait until it's over."

"There!" she said, adding some minty fresh spikes to my bangs. I looked around her into the mirror and tried to pull some hair back over my ears. She spanked my hand away. "Stop it! You'll ruin it." She smoothed my hair back into place. "I don't know why you have to be so sensitive about your ear. It's not that much bigger than the other one, really. It's just—" She broke off, studying me. "It's just that it sticks out so much." She grinned, as a red flush crawled up my neck. "You know what Mom says—"

"I *know* what Mom says," I yelled, shoving Maxey out of the bathroom. "It means I'm a 'world-class-listener.'" I slammed the door in her face.

Maxey went on outside the door, mimicking Mom's voice. "God doesn't make mistakes. If he chose to point one of your ears out, then it must mean you're destined to be a great listener—maybe a psychiatrist, or even a spy!"

"Maxine Maloney, get away from that door right now and get ready for school," Mom shouted up the stairs.

I locked the door and sighed hard. I'd never get a good partner for Discovery Project looking like this. I pulled a baseball cap from the back of the bathroom door and tried to stuff my hair under it. It only looked worse. I didn't want Mom to see it before I left the house. She'd probably make me stop and wash it, and then Maxey would get in trouble. And if Maxey got in trouble, you could bet I'd pay for it later. I scratched my head hard through my cap. Maybe I could tell everyone in class I was testing a new mint-flavored lice medicine that I invented. Our teacher said our project should be an exciting discovery or an invention that will help kids.

The prize was two tickets to the Museum of Science and Invention in Rockdale. The two kids who won got to take a whole day off school and be driven to Rockdale by a teacher chaperone. And got free lunch tickets, too, at Einstein's Cafe at the museum. I'd eaten there only once before and I wanted to go back. If you ordered hot chocolate, you got a little silver tray with a tiny cup of chocolate chips, extra whipped cream, and a peppermint stick to put in your cocoa.

Some of the most famous best friends at St. Dominic's started out as Discovery Project partners. If I could get Aurora Triboni to be my partner, we could be friends for life. She was the biggest girl in class and had some black hairs growing from her underarms already. I was wild to be friends with her. Aurora and her best friend, Kayla Quintana, split up last month at a slumber party. I hadn't had an official best friend since Lola Jo moved to Pensacola two years ago. Some of the kids were kinda funny toward me on account of my dad, but I was almost used to that. I had so many secrets saved up to tell a new best friend that I was about to explode.

And one giant one about Grandpa that I was dying to tell someone. Anyone but Mom.

I ran a dry toothbrush through my mouth quick. I figured I could skip the toothpaste today since I had half a tube on my head. Maxey's neon yellow toothbrush sat alone in a cup on the sink. I picked it up, made a silent wish, and tossed her brush into the toilet, like a coin. For luck.

Chapter 2

Maxey and I waited at the bus stop, still out of breath. For three long blocks we lugged: our lunches with Mom's special meat loaf, schoolbooks, a three-pound tin of Ginger Doodles for Mimi the crossing guard, and Maxey's giant science project. When the bus pulled up, Maxey jumped on, leaving me to carry everything.

"I'll run on and get us good seats, Effie," she called over her shoulder.

I loaded up like a pack mule while others crowded into the bus. I was the last one on, staggering, my armpits itchy with sweat. Maxey waved her pinky at me as I lumbered down the aisle. "Sorry, Ef. There weren't any seats left together."

Of course, she'd found one for herself right next to her best friend, Philomena Finch. They were already busy putting on the makeup Maxey had smuggled out of the house. Philomena Finch's little sister, Trinity, sat in the seat behind them, her nose in the Bible. You never saw her without it. She had her Notre Dame baseball cap pulled low over her eyes. She was in my fourth-grade class. Not that you'd ever notice, though. She was so quiet you could forget she was there. Everybody called her Holy Ghost, or HG for short—except in front of the teachers. I tried to remember to call her Trinity to her face, but she was always HG in my head.

She looked up at me when I passed and gave me a small smile. I was the only kid in class she paid much attention to. I guess because our sisters were best friends. I was always friendly back, but she kinda spooked me.

There was only one seat left on the bus, as always, next to Marcus Crenshaw, the most famous boy in the sixth grade. He made a living at school doing weird stuff for money and was trying to see how long he could grow his toenails. Most kids were too grossed out to sit by him. This week he'd been working on a booger collection, which was stuck to the outside of his lunchbox. He'd let you see it for fifty cents.

"Hey, Ef," he said as I sat down. "Check it out." He knocked on the outside of his lunchbox, which was now wrapped in a heavy plastic bag. To protect his collection, I guess. "I've got about forty of 'em now. And you know that kid with the big neck, Buzz? He said if I bought him some cupcakes today, he'd give me a booger. Cool, huh?"

"Swell," I said, scooching to the far side of my seat. From the aisle, I could see Maxey tossing her hair back in the way she thinks makes her look really glamorous. I gave my seatmate a long look. "Marcus, did you know my big sister, Maxey, has a crazy, mad crush on you?"

He raised his eyebrows, definitely interested. "Yeah?"

I looked down a moment at his lunchbox, feeling my breakfast threaten to come back up. "Mmm-hmm. And I bet if you go sit by her at lunch, she might have a little something for you to add to your collection."

. . .

At ten minutes to eight, we arrived at St. Dominic's. I let Marcus carry Maxey's science project off the bus. It was a model of a human heart she made with papier-mâché and spray paint. She'd labeled all the valves with little banners on toothpicks. Mom mounted it on our old Candyland game board painted green. And she lent Maxey a real stethoscope so people could listen to the *lub-dub* sound of their heart valves opening and closing. For someone who didn't actually have a heart, my sister was pretty smart about them.

Maxey and Philomena looked like they might faint when Marcus and I walked up to them. Marcus handed the heart over to Maxey and smiled as he sauntered off. "See you for lunch, eh, Maxey?"

She shoved the project back at me and spat, "Carry it. I am not touching anything Booger Boy touched."

"Maxey! I'm not carrying this all day."

"Don't be such a baby, Effie. It's just to my class." She pulled her jacket off, even though it was cold. I noticed she was wearing her best dress-up blouse, which is meant for church and not for school. It was some slinky kind of material and scoopy in front. Maxey was using a "free dress" coupon she earned for collecting the most canned goods for the missions. That meant she didn't have to wear our black and green plaid uniform for one whole day. Philomena said St. Dominic's uniforms were ugly enough to make a dog sick. I hated them because they made my backside itch after sitting in class all day.

Maxey pulled a blue jay feather out of the pocket of her blouse, which was purple and matched the eye shadow she'd put on. "I have to carry this for Mr. Constantino, and I don't want to muss it."

Mr. Constantino was her science teacher, and Maxey had plans to marry him. I once called Mrs. Constantino and warned her. She thanked me for my call and said she'd keep that in mind.

It was late when I finally reached my homeroom class with Mr. Giles, who grew hair out of his ears, instead of on his head. I always tried to speak nice and loud in case he couldn't hear me.

"SORRY I'M LATE, MR. GILES. I HAD TO STAY AND HELP MY BIG SISTER, MAXINE MALONEY." Then I dropped my voice to a loud whisper, so only those in North America could hear. "She WET HER PANTS on the bus."

Mr. Giles looked at me over the top of his glasses and cleared his throat. That was his special signal for boys and girls to stop talking and sit down. I tiptoed down the aisle to my seat, my special signal for "sorry to be late." After I sat down, I noticed he was still staring at me. He crossed his arms over his chest. That could mean anything, but mostly it meant he was waiting for me to do something else. What?

"Your hat, Effeline, please. We don't use umbrellas or hats indoors, do we?"

I slid six inches lower in my seat as I pulled my hat off. My hair was stiff and gummy, and now smashed flat against my skull. I had something that felt like a dead squirrel hanging off the back of my neck, which I was hoping was just a big wad of my gooped-up hair. (And not an actual dead squirrel.) Mr. Giles turned his back to the board, but the rest of the class kept staring at me.

"Effie!" whispered Naomi from across the aisle. "What ya got all over your hair?"

I sighed and pulled a tablet out of my desk. I printed in big letters with my thick black marker.

It's a deep condishoner because I might be going to a very fancy party tonight with a lot of rich people and my mother said I had to have it in case there are a lot of pictures being taken she doesn't want me with dry hare.

My note said, "might be going," so it wasn't an official lie. I *might* be going to the White House for dinner tonight. You just never know in life what could happen next. I held my note up to Naomi while she read it, and held it up a little longer to make sure everyone else around me had read it too.

HG gave my hair a long look and then looked away. Aurora Triboni turned around in her seat and read my note. Then shook her head. "You spelled 'hair' wrong," she whispered.

HG whipped back around. "No she didn't," she whispered back. "She used the Old English version of 'hair,' which can also be spelled h-a-r-e. You're just used to see-ing the new version." Her cheeks got very red and then she buried her head back into her Bible, which was hidden in-side her math book. HG didn't talk too much, so when she did, I think it kinda got her blood pressure up.

Aurora cocked her eyebrow up a notch and shrugged. And then turned away. Like she couldn't be bothered with this whole boring scene one more second. Not exactly a great start for two new *maybe*-best friends.

This was all Maxey's fault, I thought, steaming. She ru-ined everything. I wrote her name in big black letters across the bottom of my tablet, almost tearing through the paper. I underlined A-X-E. Figured that anybody with an "axe" right smack in the middle of their name would be hateful. I scribbled through it with sharp lines like light-ning bolts and ripped out the page. I balled it up and threw it inside my desk.

HG stole a peek at me over her shoulder, then tried to act like she hadn't.

On a clean sheet of paper, in my very best handwriting, I spelled out A-u-r-o-r-a. Then I wrote my name right next to hers. I drew a big circle around us with a line of tiny stars. We belonged together. I just knew it. And by the time the Science Olympics were over, I vowed, nothing— not even "Axey"—would be able to get between us.

Chapter 3

"Effie! Effie! Come here!" Maxey yelled at me from across the playground during afternoon recess.

I ignored her. I was trying to catch Aurora Triboni alone for one second so I could talk to her about my great idea for an invention. I was hoping she'd think it was so great she wouldn't be able to say no to being my partner. She was shooting hoops with a bunch of boys and I didn't want to interrupt her. Aurora took sports very seriously, especially when there were boys involved.

"*Effie!* I don't have all day."

"Wha-at?" I yelled as I ran over, keeping one eye glued on Aurora.

Maxey and Phil were stationed in their usual recess spot near the girls' restroom. The only sport they liked to play was Lipstick. "Do you have the key to the Scouts treasury box with you?" Maxey asked.

"Of course," I said. "It's Friday, and we always have our meeting on Fridays, and it's my responsibility—"

"Fine!" she said, cutting me off. She dug her hand down the front of my blouse.

"Hey! What ya doing?" I cried, trying to shake her off. "Stop it, Maxey!"

"Well, give it over, will you?" she said, still digging around inside my shirt. "I need to borrow it a sec. Where's that chain you wear?"

I pulled back hard and yanked myself away. "I don't have it on a chain anymore!"

Maxey sneered at me over her pointy nose. "I bet you lost it, didn't you? I knew you would sooner or later. I don't know why they ever voted you as the treasurer. You lose everything."

"I did not lose the key to the treasury!" I said. "And I don't lose everything. I only lost our church money that *one* time," I said, "and it was an accident." I looked at Phil and tried to explain. "I couldn't find my church purse on Sunday. So, I stuck the money in the pocket of my dress, but I found out it wasn't like a real pocket for putting stuff in, it was one of those fake dress pockets for just looking fancy. They're no good for holding anything. So it must have slipped out somewhere."

Phil flipped her hair and looked over her shoulder to see if anyone interesting was looking at her.

Maxey got in my face. "If you didn't lose the key, then give it. I need it for *official* school business," she said.

I licked my lips, nervous, then took a quick look over at the hoops. Oh, no! Kayla Quintana was standing just outside the court watching Aurora. She was probably going to try to get Aurora to be her Discovery Project partner. Maxey turned to see what I was looking at.

"Maxey, I have to go! I'm not giving you the key. I'm not allowed!" I started to walk away, but she pulled me back with cold, snaky fingers.

She put her face right up to mine—so close I could smell the horseradish from her meatloaf sandwich. "You lost the key, didn't you, Ef?"

"I didn't lose it! It's right—" I looked around real quick to make sure no one was looking and lifted my shirt up just a tiny bit in front. "Right here," I whispered, pointing to a big gray square on my belly. "Under the duct tape."

"You taped it to your stomach?" Phil asked, peering over Maxey's shoulder. "Gawd, you are such a freak, Effie." She elbowed Maxey. "She's almost as bad as Trinity."

"I am not!" I said. "I just didn't want to lose the key and the chain broke and I couldn't find another one."

"Okay, fine—whatever," Maxey said. "Hand it over. I need to borrow it for just a sec so I can make some change. You go play with your little friends over there, and I'll be back in five minutes."

"Go get change at the office, Maxey! I'm not letting you open the treasury!"

"They only have change for a twenty and I have a fifty. I already asked them. Right, Phil?"

She nodded and popped her gum near my ear.

"Where did you get a *fifty,* Maxey?" I asked, shocked. I'd never even seen a real fifty-dollar bill in my whole life.

"Principal Obermeyer gave it to me. She wants to buy

something at the pep club booth after school, but she is very busy and doesn't have time to go herself."

"Lemme see it," I said. "I don't believe you."

Maxey rolled her eyes at Philomena, and then looked back at me with her fake patient look. "I don't have it yet. She told me to go get some change first. Of course, I can always go back and tell her that my little sister, Effeline Maloney, treasurer for the Scouts, is refusing to give the principal change!"

I lowered my eyes to hide my fear. Ms. Obermeyer was our new principal and I'd only seen her at assembly. She had excellent posture and walked very fast. Maxey said that was because she used to be in the army. If you got in trouble, she'd make you do sit-ups and push-ups until you could just barely walk. Maxey said Billy Martindale threw up from it, and then Principal Obermeyer made him clean it up with a toothbrush. I definitely did not want to talk to her. She might make us do a hundred push-ups just for interrupting.

"Go, go, Aurora! Woo! Woo!"

My head whipped back around to the court. Kayla was bouncing under the basket doing cheers for Aurora. She was trying to move right back in on Aurora. I had to get to her before it was too late. I was torn right in two, straight up the middle. I really should go and get the change for Maxey and Principal Obermeyer myself, just to be safe. Our Scout leader, Sister Lucille, made me promise that I would never let anyone except her and me open the treasury box. But if I didn't get over to Aurora before recess was over, I might lose her to Kayla. I reached up under my shirt, ripped the tape off my stomach, and peeled two keys off the back.

"Here," I snapped. "The big key is for the supply closet and the little one is for the lockbox. When you're done, make sure you lock both—"

"Don't sweat it, Effie! You worry too much. I'll give them back to you at Scouts. Promise!"

The school bell blasted, ending recess. I raced toward the court to grab Aurora just for a minute. As she sank a neat hoop shot, Kayla and I plowed right into each other. "Oh! Sor-r-ry!" I said, trying to get my breath back.

"Watch it, Ef-fe-liiine!" she said, her face cross. Kayla always made my name sound like some terrible dental disease.

"Aurora! Can I talk to you for a sec?" I asked.

Kayla coiled herself around Aurora's arm like a snake, putting herself right in the middle of us. "What ya want?" she asked. "Need to borrow a pen to write your dad in the—"

"Shut up, Kayla!" Aurora said, giving her an elbow jab. She wiped the sweat off her face with her forearm and looked at me, curious. "What?" she asked.

"I was just wondering if you had someone to, well, um . . ." I paused, then moved closer so Kayla couldn't hear.

Kayla stuck her face right between ours. She had the meanest-looking mouth I'd ever seen—all skinny and sharp. "Can *we* help you with something, Effeline?"

"Uh, well, oh, nothing, I guess," I said, shrugging and backing off. "I'll catch you later, Aurora." No way I was going to ask her in front of Kayla.

Kayla gave me a dirty look and dragged Aurora away quick like she was some kind of celebrity .

I'd just lost my big chance. I was burning daylight—and the bats were circling, Grandpa would say. I hurried back to homeroom and rubbed the raw place on my stomach where I'd pulled the tape off. It was cold and sticky and matched the nervous feeling that slithered right across the back of my neck.

HG appeared by my side in the spooky way she had. Geez, you never saw that girl coming. "Effie," she said in her mini-ghost voice. "I was wondering if you'd picked someone for your Discovery Project, yet—'cos if you haven't, maybe you'd want to—"

I cut her off quick before she could finish. I did not want to have to turn her down, but no way did I want her for my partner. She probably had learned how to part the Red Sea like Moses and was planning to do a live demonstration for class.

"Oh, yeah! I got a great partner—but we're keeping it a secret, for fun, you know? Uh-oh! There's Mr. Giles! C'mon—we better hurry!" I dove into my desk and slid down in my seat. HG turned back around as she put her hat under her seat. She didn't look at me, but I could feel her hurt hanging in the air around me. I made a mental promise to do something really nice for her soon. Maybe leave some cookies in her desk or sit by her on the bus on purpose instead of ignoring her.

And, almost as if she heard my thoughts, right before my eyes, HG's ears grew bright red.

Chapter 4

At a quarter past three, Sister Lucille brought the weekly meeting of the St. Dominic's Angel Scouts to order. She, Father McCabe, and our mothers were the only ones who actually called us Angel Scouts. We preferred just plain "Scouts." It was bad enough that we had little feathery white wings on our beanies. I kind of liked them until I marched in our first Christmas parade next to the public school kids. They nearly bust a gut laughing at us.

"Girls! Girls!" Sister said, clapping her big, chapped hands together. "Settle down now! We've got a very full meeting today. Father McCabe will be stopping by in just a bit to show us his slides of the missions in Guatemala. Then we've got to plan our special holiday project for the poor."

I adored Sister Lucille. She had crazy red hair like mine. When I was a first grader, she let me peek up under her stiff white nun wimple to see it. Maxey said Sister Lucille was on official nun probation and might lose her job for flirting with the priests. But Maxey could be making that up because she knew I liked Sister Lucille.

"Effeline, let's take roll quickly—just an informal head count is fine, and then we'll move into our program."

"Yes, Sister, but don't forget we have to collect dues for this month," I said, jumping up. "We were supposed to do it last week, but you took us out visiting at the nursing home and we didn't get back in time."

"Oh! Dues—that's right. How could I have forgotten?" She put her finger over her lips. "I'm afraid, though, that we are on a very tight schedule today. We mustn't keep Father waiting. Perhaps we could just take roll for now?"

"But I brought my money today, Sister!" Dana Abercrombie said.

"Me too!" several other girls chimed in.

"Angels, if we have time, we'll collect dues later."

"I'll just get the roll sheet then, Sister," I said. "It'll only take a second." I jumped up from my place in Hallelujah Circle and dashed over to the supply closet. It wasn't that I was so hot about taking roll, I just wanted to make sure the lockbox was okay. It would be just like Maxey to leave it open. I'd been holding the keys so tight since Maxey gave them over after school that I had little key engravings in the palm of my hand.

I loved being treasurer. Mom was so proud of me when I got elected. I had a hunch that Sister Lucille had something to do with me winning the election. She probably got all her nun friends to stuff the ballot box in my favor. I think it was their way of trying to show everyone that it didn't matter to them about my dad, and that they could trust a Maloney kid.

I hummed under my breath to the Angel Scout song they were singing while I opened the closet door. The treasury box with angel stickers all over the lid was right where it was supposed to be—phew!

I put the small key in the padlock and pulled the lid open.

A little chill crawled up my back. The ledger card sitting on top showed our balance of $87.75—but the card was sitting very, very low in the box. I lifted the card up, then stared at the three quarters and stubby pencil sitting all alone at the bottom.

My short life passed before my eyes.

I blinked and looked again. The cash was *gone*! There was no fifty-dollar bill from Principal Obermeyer, no familiar wrinkled one-dollar bills, no fives, no tens. Just three shiny quarters. We'd been robbed! I tried to drag in a breath of air, but it felt like an elephant was sitting on my chest. This had to be a joke—Maxey and Phil's idea. I could just hear them plotting. *Hey, Phil, want to see my little sister go totally psycho at the Scout meeting?*

I licked my lips and stuck my head out the closet door. The group had finished their song and everyone had their heads bowed for the opening prayer. All except Maxey, who was eyeballing the closet door. I gave her my meanest, maddest look and motioned her to come over right *now*.

She closed her eyes and started praying with the group all of a sudden.

I cleared my throat, but she ignored me. I coughed three times—she kept praying. God was probably stunned, since I'm pretty sure He hadn't heard from Maxey in a long time. I coughed like I had a chain saw caught in the back of my throat.

"Effeline!" Sister Lucille called over to me. "Are you all right? I'll be right there—"

I jammed the lock back on the treasury and clicked it closed.

Maxey leapt up, making a quick sign of the cross. "I'll take care of it, Sister. Sometimes she just needs a good whack on the back." She hurried over and took my arm. She pulled me back into the closet and walloped me a good one between the shoulder blades.

"Ou-u-uch!" I cried in my loudest whisper.

"Well, what are you bugging me for?"

"Like you don't know!" I said, feeling crazy inside. "Where's the *money*? I want it all back right this second, Maxey!"

She glared at me, her eyes like mean little marbles. "Just shut up, Effie! It's only a few bucks. Big flipping deal! I'll have it back to you by next week. I really needed it for something. No one will ever know. If you want, I'll pay the treasury an extra dollar for interest."

"A few bucks?" I hissed. "You call eighty-seven dollars a few bucks? You could go to prison for that, just like—"

"Eighty-seven dollars? What are you talking about? I borrowed twenty bucks. That's all that was in there. And some quarters."

"You're lying! And you told me you were going to make change for Principal Obermeyer!"

She shrugged. "Well, okay, I made *that* part up! I knew you wouldn't loan me any money out of the box if I asked. All I did was come in here, open the box, and take four fives out. Then I locked up the box, locked the closet door, and gave the keys back to you after last period."

"But all the money is *gone,* Maxey! I know you took it and I want it back NOW!" I sputtered, spit flying everywhere.

She clapped her hand over my mouth and dragged me deep into the corner of the closet. She whispered right down my ear canal, her breath hot. "Just-shut-up-right-now, or everyone is going to hear!"

Sister Lucille poked her head around the corner. "Girls! What's going on here? Is everything all right?" She looked at the treasury box, which I held clutched to my chest.

"We're fine, Sister!" Maxey said, slightly loosening the choke hold she had on me. "Sometimes when Effie can't stop coughing, Mom and I have this special way of helping her. We hold her real close and help her do some deep breathing. She looked down at me. "You feeling better now, Effie?" she asked me in a sweet voice I hardly recognized.

I cleared my throat. "Yes! Thanks!"

"Well," Sister said, glancing at her watch. "Hurry along, you two! Let's take roll before Father McCabe arrives. Just leave the treasury in here for now, all right?"

"Right!" I squeaked. "I—I—I didn't even open it!"

Maxey shoved me out in front of her. "Keep your mouth shut or you'll never see fifth grade," she muttered.

I sat down at the small desk next to the Hallelujah Circle. Maxey sat back down next to Phil and kept a hard eye on me. I scraped my front teeth back and forth over my bottom lip—a nervous habit that Mom was hoping I'd outgrow.

"Effeline?" Sister Lucille said, gently prompting me to begin. "Do you have your roll sheet?"

"Uh, yes, Sister!" I reached into my backpack and pulled out my Angel Scout folder. "I had it in here all the time. I don't know why I thought it was in the closet. Dana Abercrombie?" I called, trying my best not to shriek.

"Here!" she said. She waved a ten-dollar bill over her head. "I'm paying for two months, so I don't need change today."

"Okay! I said. "But just hang on to it for now."

"Maya Bentley?" I called.

"Here!" She jumped up from the circle and came over to the desk. "I need change. My mom only had a ten. I need five back."

"Girls!" Sister Lucille called out. "We're not doing dues right now. Let Effie get through roll call."

I took a big gulp of air. "Ginger Cohen?"

"Here! And, I'll need change for a twe-e-e-nty today when you're re-e-eaaaady for it," she sang.

The classroom door flew open and Father McCabe rolled in on the back of a cart with a slide projector sitting on top. "Greetings, my beautiful Angel Scouts," he boomed. He jumped off the cart and gave a big bow. "*And my beautiful Angel Scout Leader!*" he said, giving Sister Lucille a big toothy smile.

She ducked from our view and got busy setting up chairs so we could all see better.

"He-e-llllo, Fa-ther!" we all chanted.

Sister Lucille dimmed the lights as he launched into his talk. He had one of those remote-control clickers on his slide projector that just seemed to thrill the heck out of him. Father McCabe loved the missions like some men loved fancy cars or golf or racehorses. Once you got him started, he could barely be stopped. I looked at the clock. It was already twenty-five minutes to four. If we could keep him going until a quarter past, I'd be safe.

Maxey was watching Father McCabe, I noticed, and not the slides. Maxey loved men, even priests, as much as Father McCabe loved the missions.

For the next half hour, my mind was blurred with visions of near-naked children eating white rice and oatmeal with their fingers, and crying babies getting shots in their behinds from white people with giant white smiles. In between Father McCabe's slides, I'd see ones of me and Maxey sitting near naked in a small prison cell eating rice with our fingers. I shuddered and tried to close my eyes to it, but I couldn't get rid of the picture.

I felt a pair of eyes on me and turned. HG was staring at me, like maybe she was seeing the same pictures I was. Then she pointed to her mouth and then at me. I put my hand to my mouth and it was wet. She scooted over to me and handed me a tissue. "You're bleeding," she said, her voice soft.

"Thanks," I said, and tried to blot the blood off. Mom would have a fit when she saw me like this. I hadn't done my lip bad enough to make it bleed since Grandpa had died.

The lights flipped back on, blinding us all. Sister Lucille pulled up the shades. "Father, that was wonderful! Thank you for coming to share that with us. We're going to look at some fun photos of our last Angel fund-raiser; then we've got some marvelous snacks to share while we plan our holiday project for the poor. We hope you'll stay!"

"And don't forget about dues!" Maya called.

"Sister! Sister!" I said, jumping up. "I was hoping we could have some time to um, uh, ask Father some questions. Gosh, I've got a gazillion questions about the missions."

"Me too, Sister!" Maxey piped up.

"Well, all right, girls!" she said, thrilled at our interest. "It looks like everyone is here, so we don't need to finish calling roll."

"Eff-e-liinnne, I still need ch-a-ange for a twenty!" Ginger sang.

"Sister?" HG said, climbing to her feet and raising her hand. "I have an idea."

"Yes, Trinity?" Sister Lucille said, trying to hide the surprise on her face. I don't think HG had ever talked in Scouts before. She just came because her mother made her.

27

"I think we should just all give our dues today to Father McCabe for the missions in Guatemala," she said in a rush.

Maxey jumped up. "Great idea!" She plucked Phil's beanie from her head. "I'll second that."

Father McCabe beamed and gave us all an extra blessing while Maxey went around the circle and stood in front of each girl until she dropped her money into the hat. No one was going to argue with Maxey about this. By the time she got to Ginger and Maya, there was enough to make change right out of the hat.

I was saved, for the moment, at least. But I still had eighty-seven big problems that were not going away anytime soon. And one big sister who was going straight to hell—but *not* until she paid the treasury back.

Chapter 5

After some really bad snacks—health nut bars that weighed a pound each and tasted like earwax—I snuck away and sat in a bathroom stall. I was waiting for twenty past four so I could get on the bus and go home. I wasn't going to go back into the Scout meeting and take any chance that Sister Lucille would want to check the ledger to see if it was time for us to make a deposit at the bank.

I was in trouble with a capital "T." Up to my armpits in alligators, like Grandpa would say.

I knew I had to tell on Maxey, but if I did, it would probably send Mom right over the edge. She was used to Maxey screwing up, but this was the worst ever. If she found out that Maxey had stolen money from the St. Dominic's Scout treasury, it would do her in. Chances were she'd pack her bags and just drive off and leave us. Just like Aunt Irene said Mom wanted to after she first found out about Dad six years ago.

Mom had just gotten back to kinda acting like her old

self when Grandpa died last year. It about did us all in. He'd been our main guy ever since Dad left. He fixed things around the house, made us laugh till our sides ached, took us out for fancy dinners whenever he could, and when she wasn't looking, he'd stuff Mom's wallet with cash from his Social Security check.

Then she'd stuff it back in his jacket pocket when he wasn't looking because she was too proud, is what Maxey would say.

All the brightness got sucked right out of our lives when he died. Grandpa lived his life like it was one big adventure. Like the time he got knocked clear out of a tree by lightning and didn't die or anything. It was my favorite story. I'd make him tell it to me over and over.

He said back when he was just a boy, he was out playing in the woods one day when a fierce storm barreled down— a blue norther—just the kind that Tyler Wash is famous for. He said the lightning and thunder were flashing and booming at the same time, which meant he was squat in the middle of it. He knew he should get home, but if he did, his mom would make him get away from the windows and not let him watch. And my grandpa loved a good storm! So he climbed up into a tree and tried to make himself real small so he wouldn't be such a target. Well, it rained and hailed and crackled and thundered all around him. And then it got quiet for one long Texas second, he'd say. Then the hairs on his head stood straight up and his hands started to tingle. And ka-*BLAM* went the lightning and hit the tree and split a branch right off—the very one he was sitting on. He fell off and landed right in the mud.

And I'd always say, "Grandpa, you could have been *killed*!" And he'd always say, "*That* one didn't have my name on it, Ef. I knew it sure, even back then."

The one that finally did have his name on it was a flash called Stroke and it took him fast and merciful. When Grandpa's housekeeper came the next morning, he was lying on the floor next to his bed with his ancient cat, Pretty Girl, sitting right on top of him like a big fluffy cake ornament.

I made a silent prayer to Grandpa, even though Sister Lucille said you couldn't really pray to dead relatives for things—though you could say hello. But Sister Lucille didn't know Grandpa. If there was a way he could help me, I just knew he would. I'd wait until I got home so I could pray to him in person. Well, almost in person.

The stall door next to me banged shut. I lifted my feet up and sat cross-legged on the seat. I didn't want anyone to know where I was right now. I leaned over to see whose feet they were. Big black tennies that looked kind of familiar.

I listened as my bathroom neighbor pulled a toilet-seat cover from the box on the wall. Whoever it was had nice hygiene manners, as Mom called it. I could hear the careful *r-r-rip* as she punched out the little donut hole in the middle.

"Dangnammit!" she swore. I heard her ball up the toilet-seat cover and throw it into the very short white trash can on the floor.

She pulled a fresh one from the wall dispenser. It got real quiet for a minute, and I heard the first trickle hit the paper. I have excellent hearing for these kinds of things. The tissue started crackling again. "Christopher Columbus!"

I caught my breath and held it. It was Aurora Triboni! She'd made that the new cool thing to say after we learned about the bad stuff Columbus did to the Native Americans. The nuns didn't mind because they said it in *Little Women,* too.

I heard her jump off the seat and turn, tennies facing the toilet. A pair of bright blue panties came sliding down her legs like firemen down two long poles.

"Dang stupid thing!" she whispered. A tissue storm broke out in her stall, with a lot of scrunching, tearing, and ripping.

"I hate those things too," I said finally, when it quieted down. "They just never stay put."

"Yeah, no kidding. Who is that over there, anyway?" she asked.

"It's me, Aurora—Effie." I licked my lips. Come on, girl, I told myself. Here's your chance. Just ask her! But what if she thought my idea was stupid?

"Oh, hey, Ef," she said, and sighed. I heard her sit back down hard with a clunk and probably not on a toilet-seat cover. "And if you don't get the hole torn out just right—"

"It catches there, and then you puddle up . . ."

She giggled. "Yeah, and the puddle rolls right over onto your leg."

We sighed together.

"Somebody should invent better toilet-seat covers," she said. "You could probably make a million bucks."

My heart started galloping like a wild mustang. And the world's most sensational Discovery Project idea came to me in a dazzling flash of light. I jumped down from my seat and turned to stare at the toilet lid. That's it, I thought in amazement. It would work, I just knew it!

I shivered with excitement. I could almost see the statues they'd put up in front of St. Dominic's one day of me and Aurora—famous inventors, famous rich girls, and famous best friends.

"Hey, Aurora!" I said, my voice burbling with confidence. "When you're done over there, come here a sec. I gotta show you something. I'm about to change your life."

• • •

Mom had flour all over her hands when I got home from Scouts. Pretty Girl hissed and swiped at me as I hurried by. She was still mad as heck about Grandpa up and dying on her.

"Where's Maxey, Mom?" I asked, still huffing from my run home from the bus stop. "I couldn't find her after Scouts and I waited and waited and finally I had to go or I'd miss the bus."

Mom turned around and plugged her fists into her hips. "Maxey didn't help you get on the bus?"

"No! I couldn't find her anywhere."

She gave a deep sigh but her face stayed all pinched. I knew what she was thinking. About the mean big kids who made fun of me and Maxey on the downtown bus and then made us give them all our money. It happened over two years ago, but Mom still worried about us.

"Mom, I'm fine. Nothing happened. But where is she?"

"Well, she called after Scouts and said that Mrs. Finch had invited her to come home with Phil and have dinner. I said yes, but I told her she had to first get you on the bus safely. And to make sure you were sitting by someone nice."

"Well, I didn't see her anywhere."

Mom washed her hands off quickly. "I'm going to call her right now and have her sent home."

"No, don't! Let her stay." I liked having the house to myself. I pulled my baseball cap off and dumped my backpack on the table. The stolen money would be safe over there. Mrs. Finch was really strict and I knew Maxey and Phil would have to stay home and couldn't go out shopping and spend it before I could get it back.

"Effie!" Mom said, rinsing off her hands and coming over to me. "What have you got all over your hair?" She leaned closer to sniff. "And where are those new bunny barrettes I got you?"

"Oh, uh, I left them at school in my desk. They felt kind of loose and I didn't want them to fall out," I lied before I could stop myself.

Mom pulled me over to the sink and turned on the water. "What in God's name did you put on your hair?"

"It's toothpaste. Maxey did it. It was supposed to be styling gel, except we don't have any. I tried to make her stop." I surrendered to the warm water running through my hair, and Mom massaging my scalp. That was one of the ways that Mom had changed that I missed the most. She hardly touched us anymore unless it was to clean us or feed us. Now I just kinda sucked it up when I could get it.

"Effie, you've got to learn to hold your own against her. Say no when you need to."

"She's really hard to stop, Mom," I said, thinking past the toothpaste to the keys to the treasury. I still couldn't believe she'd gotten those from me.

"Well," Mom said, "it sounds like it's time for me to put Maxey back on her success chart."

My head reared up like one of those killer whales surfacing at Sea Universe. Water flew everywhere. "No, Mom! Not another success chart," I sputtered.

"Ef-fie!" she said, pushing me back down and trying to blot us both dry with a dishtowel. "Maxey needs to be reined in from time to time. Putting toothpaste in your hair right before you go to school is completely out of line. I won't have it."

A success chart was Mom's idea of curing Maxey's bossy behavior. Maxey got stars for being "appropriate" with me, and got grounded when she wasn't. Maxey ended up getting stars for the biggest upchucking display of fake Nice Sister behavior you've ever seen. She could turn in the stars for money if she earned enough. If she blew it, she got grounded. To our room. Like where I lived. So I was the one who ended up getting punished. I asked Mom if she could ground Maxey to the backyard, but Mom said it was too cold out there. And the neighbors might complain.

Mom turned my head and ran warm water over my ears and the back of my neck. Her voice was more like a muffled hum now, but I could guess what she was saying. She was worried I'd end up like Dad. It was a sermon I'd heard plenty of times before.

She turned off the water. "—and she has such a strong personality. You're going to have to deal with people like her your whole life." She pulled me up and threw a clean dishtowel over my head. Gave my scalp a brisk rub. I watched her face as she gave my head a good going-over, as if one single drop of damp would certainly lead me straight to pneumonia. I fought an urge to lay my head on her shoulder and confess the whole sorry mess right then and there. I tried to guess what she would say. But it wouldn't be what she would say. It would be the look on her face. I took a big breath and let the moment slide away.

"Hey! Guess what?" I said, desperate to change the subject.

"Well, *what?*" she said, turning back to the bread she was making. It was her weekend therapy, she'd always say.

"Aurora Triboni is going to be my Discovery Project partner!" I said, loving the way her name just rolled off my tongue.

Mom looked over at me and gave me a small smile. "Great! She liked your idea about refizzing flat soda?"

I tried to shake some water from my ear. "Not that one. I got an even better idea today!" I was so relieved to get past the near-moment-of-confession that I sounded a little crazy, like when I'd had too much sugar. "And Aurora loved it! I bet we win best Discovery Project! Isn't that *great!*"

"So, what is it?" Mom looked intrigued.

"I can't tell you! My maybe-new-best-friend Aurora and

me agreed that it has to be top secret. We can't tell anybody. Not even mothers," I added. I took the towel from Mom and wiped my face off. "But I need to have something of yours to make our project. But I can't tell you what it is because it would be a big clue. So can I have it?"

Mom raised an eyebrow. "Now, Ef, how can I answer that?"

"You for sure don't need them anymore," I said. "And the box they come in said it only costs a dollar ninety-nine. Please, Mom, please, it's for schoooool!"

She threw up her hands. "I give! They're yours, Madame Curie. Go forth and discover!"

I ran down the hall to call Aurora, feeling like I'd been on some crazy carnival ride all day. Thrilled and sick to my stomach, all rolled up into one.

Chapter 6

At the exact stroke of midnight, my Angel Scout glow-in-the-dark alarm clock, which was buried under the covers, went off. I had set it on vibrate before I went to bed, so it didn't sing *Good morning, dear God* like it usually does. But its little wings were beating like mad against my stomach.

I jackknifed up in bed. My pajama top was all cold and wet next to my skin. I'd been having a terrible dream. Naked Guatemalan kids were skating tiny circles around me like I was some kind of Maypole. They were wrapping and unwrapping me with big rolls of duct tape. Their skates were so noisy, and Principal Obermeyer was there too. She kept yelling and shining this bright light in my eyes.

I shivered and squeezed myself. I hadn't had a nightmare about Principal for a long time. I used to have them a lot in first grade after she'd talk in assembly with her big boomy voice.

I looked over at Maxey. She was sleeping on her back with her hair fanned out perfect. Not a single tangle, I bet.

I shoved back the rats in my hair. I remembered why I'd set the alarm. I had a plan. I was either going to kill Maxey in her sleep and hope Mom wouldn't mind—or I was going to get up and take back the money Maxey stole from the treasury.

I slipped out of the covers nice and quiet and tiptoed over. She had her mouth open just a tiny bit. Some kid at camp told me once you could drown in one mouthful of water if you were asleep.

"STOP STARING AT ME, FREAK!" she yelled, rearing up.

I nearly jumped out of my flannels. "GOD, Maxey! Shut up! You'll wake up Mom—"

"I don't CARE! What the heck are you doing?" She grabbed my arm hard and pulled me toward her.

I tried to wrench away. She grabbed my collar and pulled. It tore right across.

"Look at what you did!" I cried. "You ripped it. Mom is going to kill you. These are my new ones and they were eleven ninety-nine."

She shoved me away with both hands. "Get away from me, freak."

"No!" I said, coming back at her. "I want to know what you did with the treasury money. I swear, Maxey—if you don't give it back right now, I am going to tell Mom! And where *were* you after school anyway?"

Mom came to the doorway, the hall light framing her. "It's *midnight*! What is going on in here?"

"Sorry, Mom," Maxey said. "Effie is really worried

about her Discovery Project so I was trying to get her mind off it. I told her this hilarious joke and the punch line is kind of loud. And then I was telling her how worried I was today when I couldn't find her after school."

"You couldn't find me?" I sputtered. "You're the one who left Scouts early. I stayed there and waited for fifteen whole minutes."

"Well," she said, shrugging, "I just left Scouts for a minute so I could call Mom about going home with Phil, and then when I got back and couldn't find you, I went to our special place hoping you'd be there, but you weren't."

"What special place?" I asked.

"The flagpole, silly, where else?" she said, coming over and smoothing my covers. I swear, if they ever make a movie about the Garden of Eden, they can hire Maxey to be the serpent's voice. "Effie, what did I tell you on your very first day at St. Dominic's, when you were so hysterical about starting school?"

"I was not hysterical," I huffed.

"*Remember?* I told you that if you ever get lost or scared, just go to the flagpole and wait. It's the highest point for blocks. You can see it from almost everywhere. I'll always come for you there." She looked up at Mom. "I was just sure she'd be there today."

Mom guided Maxey back to her bed and pulled the covers over her. "Get to sleep, both of you," she said in her stern coach voice. And then it softened just a tiny bit as she turned out the light. " Good night, girls. Good dreams."

A little late for that, I thought.

" 'Night, Mom," we said in unison.

I sat up to punch my pillow into shape, and it crackled. I reached underneath. My hand closed around a small cellophane bag. Ahhh, chocolate bridge mix. My favorite thing in the whole galaxy.

When Grandpa was alive, he used to hide candy for Maxey and me under our pillows. After he died, it kept showing up. I guess Mom wanted us to feel that he was still with us. She must have snuck in after I fell asleep. I shoved a big handful into my mouth, not caring that I'd already brushed my teeth. Candy, especially chocolate, always made me feel better about everything.

"Could ya gimme a break?" Maxey said, sitting up and glaring at me. Now that Mom was gone, she was back to using her regular mean voice. "You sound like you're chewing up concrete over there. I'm trying to go to sleep."

I bolted up and spit back at her, bits of chewed-up almond flying all over. "I don't know how you plan on sleeping when we are both about ready to be carted off to jail!"

"Don't be so dramatic, Effie. They're not going to send us to jail. I'll put the twenty dollars back next week, and well, you are just going to have to tell Sister Lucille that you lost the rest—because I didn't take it."

"I did *not* lose our money! It was there last Friday when I counted it, and NO one, except you, had the key until today."

"Well, doesn't Sister Lucille have a key?"

"Of course she does! But she wouldn't take any out without telling me."

"Maybe she's trying to frame you," Maxey suggested, trying to cover a yawn.

I turned my head and stared at Maxey. "Swear to me—on Grandpa's grave—that you only took twenty dollars out."

She sighed and turned away, rolling onto her side. "I already told you. I'm not swearing on anybody's grave. That's so wack!"

I got out of bed and went over to the door and closed it so Mom wouldn't hear us. I grabbed Maxey's backpack from the desk and ripped open the zipper.

Maxey leapt up, grabbed it away from me, and knuckle-socked me hard in the arm.

I had to bite my lip to keep from yelling. I tried to rub the pain out. "Fine! Then look at me straight in the eye and tell me you only took twenty dollars—swear it on Dad's life."

She grabbed me by the shoulders. "I *said* I took twenty dollars. I needed it for a big library fine. I lost a very expensive book. I didn't want to ask Mom for it because she'd have a fit. You know how she's always talking about how broke we are. I'll put it back just as soon as I can."

"But you can't just take money like that, Maxey! And besides, how are you going to pay it back, anyhow?"

"It's not stealing, Effie." She sighed and put her hand on her hip. She tried to hook my hair around my ear but I whipped my head away. "Look," she said. "Mom pays our Scout dues, right?"

"So?" I said.

"Well, I'm just temporarily borrowing the money back that our mother gave to the treasury so I can pay back the library without getting her all upset. I've got a plan to get the twenty back. So just chill, will you? The library gets what they want, Mom doesn't get her undies in a wad, and no one finds out—"

"So how are you going to get twenty dollars?" I asked.

Maxey ticked off on her fingers. "I'm selling my science project to this kid I know who goes to public school. He is a total moron and can't come up with his own. Then Holly is going to buy my old Rollerblades—and I'm doing some hair extensions for Kiera's cousin, who is fifteen."

"Why couldn't you have just got the money from all those things first, then paid the library? Why did you have to take it out of the treasury?"

"Because the librarian sent a note to Mr. Constantino about it and it was totally embarrassing. I promised him I would pay it off today. I couldn't let him down," she said, twirling a long lock of her white hair.

I changed the subject quick. I didn't want Maxey to go off to Ga-Ga Land thinking about Mr. Constantino. Her eyes would turn into spinning hearts. "Think, Maxey! Did you give the keys to anyone else? Like even for a sec?" I begged.

"Oh, sure! I passed them around during study hall and invited everyone to go help themselves to your precious little cash box."

"I'm serious! Did anyone go with you to the closet? Did you take Phil?"

"No! I made her stand outside and guard the door because Marcus Crenshaw kept following me around with that disgusting lunchbox all day."

"So both of them knew you went in there?" I asked, aghast.

"Well, yeah! But they didn't have the keys, so they certainly couldn't have gotten to the cash."

"Where were the keys all afternoon before you gave them back to me?" I asked.

"Well, I didn't tape them to my stomach, that's for sure. I put them on my key ring so I wouldn't lose them."

Which dangles off the back of her backpack, along with her pep club bells and tiny stuffed talking kangaroo. Anybody with a brain as big as an acorn could have gotten those keys. This didn't exactly narrow the search down.

It was a whole hour later before I finally fell into a deep sleep, my jaw propped open by a giant piece of chocolate bridge mix.

Chapter 7

The next morning I stood on the porch in front of Aurora Triboni's house on Langhurst Drive. My backpack was bulging with supplies and a sack lunch, just in case Mrs. Triboni didn't provide lunches. Some mothers don't. Last night Mom said I could ride my bike over because it was only two miles away.

So far no one had answered my knock, but it was early. I looked at my M&M watch, which I had earned by eating eight bags of candy and sending in $3.99. It was twenty minutes to seven. Maybe they were all still sleeping, like at my house. Maybe I'd come too early. But Aurora said to come "after breakfast." I usually have my breakfast around eight a.m. on the weekends, but just in case Aurora ate earlier, I had mine at six o'clock today and hurried right over. I had a lot of things to do this weekend. Aurora and I had to make our invention, and after that I had to figure out a way to get eighty-seven dollars back in the treasury lickety-split.

The door was yanked open by a little kid zipped up in a

yellow pajama suit, the kind with built-in feet. Except his feet were too big for it and his toes were poking through the worn-out ends. His nose was running down to about his knees. You could tell he was still too young to be answering the door, because now that he had it open, he wasn't sure what he was supposed to do next. So he just stared at me.

"Hi, kid. I'm Effeline Maloney. Is Aurora home?"

He sniffed and then exhaled, which blew a big snot bubble out of one nostril. I tried not to watch, but a thing like that just kind of captures you. When it got bigger than the rest of his nose, he swiped it with his sleeve. And then wandered away, leaving the door wide open. Which in little kid language means "come on in."

The living room was still pretty dark except for the light coming from the television. All the curtains were still closed, and I didn't smell any breakfast smells. It smelled like kids in this house. Like a whole herd of them lived here.

"Aurora?" I whispered, in no particular direction. "It's Effie. Are you home? Aurora?" Mom has been teaching me about being patient. I figured I should wait quietly, so I wouldn't disturb anyone until they woke up.

I sat on the corner of the couch and opened my backpack. Checked my list again to make sure I had all my supplies for our Discovery Project.

1. Butcher paper.
2. Scissors, two pairs, in case Aurora doesn't have any.

3. Small plate for tracing.
4. Glue stick.
5. One box Stay-Sure Mini-pads.

My stomach growled, even though I'd already had my breakfast. I reached into my lunch bag for something to munch on. Kid Triboni looked up from the TV when he heard the crackling of my paper sack. He toddled over and stood at my knee, peering into my backpack. "Cook-kie?" he asked, hopeful.

"No, not cookie—medicine. Very bad medicine." I made a face like I'd just tasted spoiled tuna fish, and shoved my sack back into my backpack. It's not that I'm stingy or anything, I just didn't want him to snot up my lunch.

In Scouts we were learning about how you should always share, even when you don't think you have enough. Like the time that Jesus fed a whole hill full of people with just a few old fish and some bread. Not to be disrespectful to Jesus or anything, but I think the trick there was his passing out uncooked fish and old bread. People were probably just being polite and passing it on to the next person. Now, if he'd handed out pizza or something good, feeding a whole crowd would have been a real miracle in my book.

The clock above the Tribonis' dining room table bonged seven o'clock on the dot. Surely Mom would think I'd been patient enough.

"Hey, kid, which one is Aurora's bedroom?"

He plugged his mouth with his thumb and pointed toward the hallway with his other hand. He turned back to the television, his eyes shiny with cartoon fever.

There were a lot of doors in the hallway and they didn't have names or anything on them. I knocked on the first door, very soft and polite. I heard a muffled reply, which might have been Aurora saying something to me, so I went right in.

Mrs. Triboni with very messy hair looked up from under the covers. Mr. Triboni was still dead asleep, but one eye was half open with the eyeball rolled back.

I tiptoed toward the bed with my best manners. "Good morning, Mrs. Triboni," I whispered. "I'm Effeline C. Maloney. Nice to meet you."

She rubbed her eyes and perched herself up on one elbow. She pulled the covers to her chin with one hand and reached for her glasses with the other. Then she looked me up and down in a not very polite way that Mom says you're not to do when you're talking to someone.

"You're WHO?" she asked, not whispering, looking at me over the top of her glasses.

Mr. Triboni snorted real loud, and I almost jumped out of my skin. He sounded like one of those big pink hogs at the county fair during feeding time. Mrs. Triboni slapped him on the shoulder, and he rolled over.

I moved closer to the bed, keeping a careful eye on Mr. Triboni. "Eff-e-line," I repeated, real slow this time. "I'm going to be Aurora's new best friend. Well, I hope I'm going to be," I added. "It's not for sure yet."

"Why are you in my bedroom?" she asked, her voice scratchy like she hadn't had a drink of water in about a week.

"I'm looking for Aurora. We're supposed to work on our Discovery Project this morning, only when I came over, everybody was still in bed. Except for your little boy. He let me in," I explained. "I waited very patiently in your living room for twenty minutes."

Mrs. Triboni fell back hard on her pillow. "Across the hall, second door on the left. And tell Aurora to turn on the coffee."

"Thank you, Mrs. Triboni. It's very nice to meet you. You have very pretty pajamas," I added. Actually, they were about as worn out as Aurora's little brother's pajamas. And one of Mrs. Triboni's b-o-o-b-s was trying to get out near a missing button in front. But Mom says it's nice to compliment people about one thing when you first meet them. Since I was staring at her top, it was the first thing I could think of to say.

She pointed toward the door and rolled over, muttering.

• • •

Aurora poured a black mountain of coffee into the filter, scratched her hip, and threw the power switch. She pulled a stack of chipped cereal bowls from the cupboard and dumped them onto the table.

"Bradley! Get in here!" She ripped a wad of paper towels from the dispenser. She waited about twenty seconds and then sighed real loud. "Scuse me," she said.

She returned a minute later with Bradley under one arm and dumped him up on the kitchen counter. She held the paper towels over his face. *"Blow!"* she said.

He blew a tiny gust.

"No, Brad-ley, *bl-o-o-www!*"

He blew again, like a flea exhaling, and tried to wiggle off the counter.

Aurora pinned him back in place and stuck her face up into his. "Give it to me, Bradley, like you're the Mighty Lizard Boy Avenger! You're going to *blow* the Evil Horned Turtle Man right off the planet."

Bradley lifted his shoulders, stuck out his chest, and nearly blew his brains out.

Aurora mopped up the goopy mess on his face. "Good boy." She helped him down to the floor. He replugged his mouth with his thumb and wrapped an arm around her leg.

"Effie, grab some milk out of the fridge, will you?" She popped some bread into the toaster, threw some spoons onto the table. Bradley remained attached to her like a third leg. "Have you had breakfast already?" she asked.

"Yeah, thanks, though," I said.

Aurora pulled a load of cereal boxes from the cupboard. Fruity Flipping O's, Chocolate Animal Flakes, Big Sugar Wheats. I licked my lips. It was the biggest collection I'd ever seen of what Maxey and I called Forbidden Flakes. Mom only bought cereal that was full of vitamins and iron. And made your mouth taste like you'd just licked someone's hammer.

"But I didn't eat much," I explained. "I could eat some cereal to keep you company."

"Sure, help yourself." She peeled Bradley off her leg, tucked a napkin under his chin, and poured some cereal into his bowl. In her own, she poured some from each box, the prettiest sight I'd ever seen. I almost drooled right onto the table. And then copied her bowl exactly, like I did this every day. A luscious scent of fruit, chocolate, and sugar hung over the table.

"Where's the rest of the kids?" I asked, hoping no one could hear the sound of my taste buds exploding. "Aren't there more?"

Aurora wiped the milk beard growing on Bradley. "Yeah, I got four more brothers," she said, counting them on her fingers. "Flint's the oldest, then Chip, Buck's the third, then Beau. He likes to write his name B-o-w, like in 'bow and arrow,' but it's really spelled the old-fashioned way, B-e-a-u. He gets teased about it a lot. Anyway, they're all gone this weekend. Some Wolf Scout survival trip. So me and the Brad Man here are running the show, aren't we, buddy?"

Bradley rocked to his chewing and wove a little wet nest in the top of his hair with sticky fingers.

"Five brothers!" I sighed. "You're lucky! I wish I could have *one*. I just have a sister, and she's mean as a snake."

Aurora shoved a spoonful of cereal into her mouth and shook her head. When she could speak, she said, "I'd give anything to have a sister, even a mean one!" She brought her bowl to her mouth and drained the milk. Mom would have fallen right out of her seat over that one. I lifted my bowl and did the same.

Aurora wiped her mouth on the front of her pajamas. "I don't have anyone to help me around the house. My mom works like a dog at her job, so everything kind of falls on me. My dumb brothers know everything about how to live in the wilderness. But do you think they know anything about living indoors?"

"No?" I asked, hoping this was the right answer.

"*No* kidding! They can trap and skin a rabbit and make a shelter out of twigs, but do you think they can make their own sandwich for school? Or change their own sheets?"

"I bet they can't!" I said, caught up in her huff.

"When I get married and have sons," she continued, "they can't join Scouts until they can clean a house, buy a week's worth of groceries, make a meal, and"—she stopped and sniffed over toward Bradley—"and change a kid's diapers."

I didn't even need to sniff. The Brad Man had definitely been working on some kind of project in his diaper.

"That's why I wish I had a sister," Aurora said with a loud sigh. "So I could have someone to help me out. And talk to me about girl things, you know? My ex–best friend Kayla has three sisters, no brothers. Man, I loved going over to their house," she said, a dreamy look settling on her face.

I tried for a moment to imagine having three Maxeys at home to deal with. I shuddered. "Are they big sisters or little sisters?" I asked.

"All younger," she said.

"Well, there you go," I said, resting my case. "Little sisters are kind and helpful. Having a big sister is like having the school bully living right in your house. And your mom doesn't get it because she's blinded by motherly love."

"Hey, watch it, there!" Aurora said. "I'm a big sister, you know!"

"Yeah, but you're different," I said, thinking of how she'd fixed Bradley his breakfast and helped the Mighty Lizard Boy Avenger blow his nose. "You look out for him. When I was a kid, Maxey was constantly plotting to screw me up. You know what she used to tell me when I was little?"

Aurora buttered a piece of toast with nearly half a cube of butter, then shoved it into her mouth. "What?"

"She told me that if I woke up ever and saw the Tooth Fairy, the Easter Bunny, or Santa, my eyeballs would explode and I'd be left with burnt-out sockets." I shook my head, still mad.

"Most kids," I went on, "are excited to go to sleep on Christmas Eve, or before Easter, or with a tooth under their pillow—me, I was a nervous wreck. For years I'd go to bed with my bathrobe belt tied around my eyes for protection," I said.

"Man, that is mean. How'd you finally figure out it wasn't true?" Aurora asked.

The coffeemaker gurgled behind us. "Whoops! Forgot Mom's coffee," Aurora said. She jumped up and poured a quick cup, adding a splash of milk from Bradley's training cup. Along with a load of backwash and one Fruity Flipping O.

I jumped up. "I can change Bradley's diaper while you're doing that!"

"Okay," she said, tossing me a clean diaper from the counter. "Just make sure that when you're done, Bradley says thank you, and then you give him the dirty diaper to carry to the trash can." She rumpled his hair. "I'm training this one different."

As I scooped Bradley out of his booster chair, the smell hit me smack in the face. Like a barnyard gone bad.

"Bradley stinky pants?" he asked, petting my eyebrow.

"Big stinky pants," I agreed, trying to talk and hold my breath. But it was worth it. By the end of this day, I plotted to myself, Aurora was going to wonder how she'd ever lived without me.

Chapter 8

"Okay, I think we got a good one," I said. "Let's go try it out!"

It had taken us all morning, but we'd finally come up with one perfect kid-friendly toilet-seat cover. It was a roomy oval with a big precut hole in the middle so you didn't have to tear that part out yourself.

We made our way across Aurora's bedroom floor, which was littered with balled-up pieces of butcher paper. They looked like giant snowballs sitting on her cotton-candy pink carpet. Aurora had one of those princess bedrooms in ruffly pink and white. Except with her living in it, it looked more like the Sports Plus store. Aurora had a lot of athletic equipment and a different pair of muddy sneakers for every sport.

Aurora held the toilet-seat cover real careful around the edges, then shoved open a door next to her room. I grabbed the rest of the supplies we would need.

"Wow! You have your own bathroom?" I whispered in my church voice.

"Yeah, my mom insisted on it when we first bought this house. She grew up sharing a bathroom with a bunch of brothers, and she didn't want me to go through the same thing."

"You are so lucky!" I breathed as we hurried in. Out of habit, I clicked the lock behind us. I was always expecting Maxey to barge in on me the minute I went into a bathroom.

Aurora lifted the toilet lid and laid our invention down on the seat. Perfect match. We both breathed a sigh of relief.

"Nice fit, huh?" I asked. "Now, let's see where we need to put the fasteners on this." I handed her a mini-pad and a glue stick. "Put one right there in the middle on your side."

Aurora made a face at the mini-pad and held it up between two fingers. "Effie, we can't use *these*. They're . . . you know, mini-pads!"

"Sure we can," I said, trying to twist the cap off the glue stick. " 'Periods are perfectly normal—nothing to be squeamish about,' " I said, quoting Mom. "And my mom can't have periods anymore so we might as well use them up."

"How come can't she have periods?"

I hesitated a moment but then went on. "My dad doesn't live with us anymore. . . ."

"Yeah, I heard about that," Aurora said, her voice careful. "Sorry, and all."

"Thanks," I said, feeling my ears get hot. "So my

mom doesn't have periods. You need a husband at home for that."

Aurora looked up from her glue stick. "Effie, you don't have to have a husband to get a period! Weren't you there when Sister Mary Michael showed us the puberty movie a few months ago?"

"I was there! I mean, I know everybody *gets* their period. But Maxey saw another movie at school that they save for *sixth* graders. They tell you a LOT more stuff that you don't know. And it's stuff that even moms aren't allowed to tell you until then."

Aurora raised an eyebrow. "Like what?"

"Well," I said, "for one, even though everyone gets a period, not everyone keeps their period. If you don't have holy sexual relations for five years, your periods just stop. That's why nuns don't have periods."

Aurora snorted. "Nuns do too have periods! I saw some nuns once shopping at Best Bargains and they had maxi-pads in their cart. I think Maxey is pulling another fast one on you, Effie. Like she did about the Easter Bunny blowing your eyeballs out. What else did she tell you was in the movie for sixth graders?"

I shrugged and got very busy putting the glue on my mini-pad. "Oh, just some stuff about sperm. I forget now, really." I wasn't going to tell her what Maxey said about sperm being manufactured from the sperm whale until I could double-check that.

"Here, like this," I instructed her, turning the mini-pad over. I smeared a big line of glue down the center of the soft side of her pad. "Now we put two of these on the toilet cover. Then, when the kid is ready to sit down, they pull off the little paper strips on the back of the mini-pads. Instant stick-o, get it?"

"Hey, let me try it, okay?" Aurora peeled the paper off the sticky strips and stuck our invention to the toilet seat. She backed up onto the seat and plopped down.

"How's it feel?" I asked, so excited that it was making me have to go to the bathroom.

"Pretty good!" She wiggled around a little. "Doesn't slide. That's good! You know," she said, "we need to test it for real. That's part of being good scientists, like Mr. Giles said."

"I'll do it," I said. "Quick, get off. I need to go real bad."

The phone in Aurora's bedroom rang. "Oh darn it," she said, backing out the door. "I'll be right back." She stuck her head back in a half second later, catching me midstream. "Do you want me to bring Beau's camera? Should we take a picture?"

"Aurora!" I shoved her head out and closed the door firmly. And finished my business. I stood up and flushed and then inspected our invention.

Still dry, not a rip, not a tear. Could probably handle another half-dozen passengers before you needed to throw it away. But mothers would never go for that.

I opened the door just a crack to see if Aurora was off the phone. She was sitting at her desk with her back to me.

"Yeah, well, I think she's pretty nice. We're just hanging out," she said into the phone.

I closed the door so she couldn't see me but kept my "outstanding" ear pressed hard against it.

"Oh, just stuff. Nothing special. What are you and your sisters doing today?" she asked.

Kayla Quintana! I bet Aurora was talking to her ex–best friend!

"No, I'm not!" she denied, her voice getting kind of hot, as if she'd heard my thoughts.

"She is not! I don't have—" She broke off. "Hey, I don't know why you should care. You're the one—"

I'm not *what,* Aurora? She's the one who did *what?* Geez, I wish she'd use whole sentences.

"Look, I gotta go. No! I already said no! It is none of your business! I gotta go. Effie is waiting for me." She sighed real loud. I could hear it through the door. "Well, maybe. I'll call you later, okay?"

I barged right back in like I didn't even know she was talking to someone. "Oh, scuse me!" I said as she hung up. "I didn't know you were still on the phone."

"It's okay," she said. "I was done."

I started cleaning up our mess nice and quiet, giving her a chance to tell me about Kayla's call. Instead, she just helped me pick up, kinda serious and clammed up all of a sudden.

"Hey!" she said, brightening. "How'd our seat cover work?"

"It worked great! Go try it. I think we can win!"

She came over and gave me a high five, which almost knocked me off my feet. I could see I was going to have to get in shape for my new best friend. She was a very strong girl.

"Sorry!" she laughed. "I'm used to doing that with my brothers."

"Now, don't forget," I warned. "This is top secret. We have five more days until it's our turn in class."

"I won't tell anyone—promise!" she said.

"You know," I said, putting my supplies away in my backpack, "maybe we should tell each other a personal secret, kind of like insurance. I'll have one on you, and you'll have one on me. That way, if you tell anyone about our toilet cover, then I get to tell everyone at school about your other secret."

"But I'm not going to tell anyone, Ef," Aurora said.

"Oh, I know, me either! That's just how insurance is. It's just in case."

Aurora plopped herself belly-down on her lacy bedspread, sweeping off a football and a flat basketball. "Okay, but you go first. I have to think of something."

I chewed the inside of my lip. "Me too," I said, dropping cross-legged onto the floor near her. For one second I thought about telling her the mess I was in with Sister Lucille and the treasury. But I just couldn't. What if she didn't believe me? What if she thought me and Maxey were just a couple of chips off the old block?

Or I could tell her my secret about Grandpa. I hadn't ever told anyone, not even Lola Jo. It wasn't something you wanted to put in a letter, even to your old best friend.

I pulled my knees up to my chin. I didn't really know

Aurora very well yet, but I wanted to be just like her. She was tall and strong and smart and funny and had her own bedroom with a matching bathroom. I wanted to sleep over a lot and have Forbidden Flakes again. I bet the Tribonis had real hamburgers for dinner, not turkey tofu ones. And, best of all, I bet that if Aurora was my best friend, Maxey would be too scared to boss me around anymore.

I refastened the Velcro on my sneakers and licked my lips. Telling Aurora a big secret like the one about Grandpa would kinda be like giving her a giant present. It would show her how much I liked her and how much I was willing to trust her. Then maybe she'd tell me her biggest secret. Something like that could seal the deal and make two girls best friends for life. Maybe we could have a special ceremony afterward and trade friendship rings. Then maybe one day I'd be able to tell her the secret about the treasury—after I'd gotten the money back from Maxey and maybe from the other kid who stole the rest—if there *was* another kid and not just Maxey lying to me.

I looked up at the bed. Aurora stared down at me. "Well?" she asked. "Did ya think of one yet?"

Win or lose her, I decided, right then and there. I was going for it. "Okay," I said, my voice tiny as Tinker Bell's all of a sudden. "I got one."

Aurora turned over onto her side, propped her head up with her fist. "Let's hear it!"

I drug up a deep breath, then just blurted it out.

"I stole my grandpa's ashes."

Chapter 9

Aurora scooched down the bed and stared over the end at me. "You did wha-a-at?" she asked.

"I stole my grandpa's ashes," I said. "You know, from when he was cremated."

"Catholics don't get cremated," she said.

"My grandpa was a Protestant," I explained. "They don't mind getting burned up at the end."

She looked at me, her eyes wide, nodding for me to go on.

"After he died," I said with a big sigh, "we had his ashes in this special vase in our house."

"An urn," she said.

"Yeah, an urn. And I really liked having them around. But then after a month, Mom said it was time to let his ashes go. She wanted to throw him in the lake! I told her that was no way to treat her father-in-law, but she said Grandpa loved the lake. She said that was where they had thrown my grandma's ashes, and it was time the two of them were together again."

Aurora chewed her thumbnail.

"Well . . ." I paused to catch my breath. "I told her that

since I was only a baby when Grandma died, I couldn't have stopped her from dumping those ashes. But, there was no way I was going to let her throw my grandpa in the lake."

I stopped to steady myself. I'd been holding this secret to myself so long, now that it was coming out, it felt like I'd just let a wild animal loose in the room. Kinda made me nervous.

"So-o-o, what happened?" she said.

"At first Mom was nice about it and kept saying she understood how hard it was to let Grandpa go. Then when it got real close to the day we were going to the lake, I took the urn and hid it. She kind of lost her patience about it then and told me the urn better be back on the mantel by Saturday morning or else."

Aurora popped a piece of gum into her mouth and offered me the pack. I took one, to save, not to chew. My first piece of gum from my (maybe!) new best friend.

"Did you put it back?" she asked, popping her gum.

"Kind of," I said. "I put the urn back, but not the ashes."

"But didn't she notice the ashes were gone?"

I pulled up my sock, all of a sudden wishing I'd started out with an easier secret.

"Effie," Aurora said, sliding off the bed and sitting down next to me. "Didn't she notice the ashes were gone?"

"Um, I used fakes."

"*Fake* ashes?" she asked, sounding pretty amazed.

"Uh-huh, I made 'em."

Aurora hooked my hair over my ear where it was hanging over my face. My "outstanding ear" was great for that. You could probably hang a sweater on it if you needed to.

"How do you make fake ashes?"

"It's easy, really," I said. "I just took a handful of kitty litter, some sand, and some tiny gray rocks from our aquarium. Mixed it all up and, well, fake ashes!"

Aurora hooted. "And that's what your mom threw in the lake?"

I nodded. "We rented a little boat and paddled out to the middle of Prospect Lake. My mom said a little prayer. Then we poured some ashes into each of our hands and threw them into the lake. Except when Maxey threw hers, a little wind came up and blew some back into her face." I enjoyed a small smile, remembering. "She was just about to pitch a fit, but Mom told her it was just Grandpa saying goodbye to her. I was dying to tell her that she had kitty litter in her hair, but I couldn't."

Aurora slapped the bed, laughing. "Omigod! I wish I could have seen that. That is so hilarious." She looked at me with bright, friendly eyes. Like she liked me a lot. "So what did you do with the real ashes?"

"I poured them into my old second-grade thermos. And hid them in my very secret hiding place."

What I didn't tell her was that sometimes I slept with my thermos.

"Wow, that's so cool," she said. "Are you going to keep him in your thermos forever?"

"I dunno," I admitted. "I haven't thought it out that far. I just knew I had to keep him out of the lake. Hey, promise!" I said, my voice stern. "You can't ever tell anyone! Especially not my sister!"

Aurora raised two fingers. "Promise."

"Pinky promise?" I said, holding out my little finger. She linked hers with mine. "Break this pinky promise, and . . ." I hesitated, trying to think of something terrible.

"Break this promise," Aurora chanted, "and I'll have to eat my lunch out of Marcus Crenshaw's special lunchbox for a week!"

We both squealed in real horror.

"Okay, so, what's yours?" I said. "You owe me a big secret." Or even a medium one, I thought. Like who you were talking to on the phone twenty minutes ago, and what do they want you to do that you don't want to do?

"Well, it's kind of embarrassing," she said, clearing her throat.

"It's okay, Aurora. You can trust me," I said, patting her knee.

She sighed. "I'm starting to grow hair under my arms already."

I looked at her, incredulous. That was her secret? Everyone in the fourth grade knew that already.

Aurora crossed her arms over her chest, her face red.

I could tell this was really hard for her. What would be even worse was if she knew that kids already knew. I guess because she was the biggest girl in class, no one had ever dared tease her about it.

"Lucky!" I breathed. "I can't wait until I get hair under my arms."

Aurora looked over at me and smiled, kinda shy. And full of relief. "Wanna stay for lunch?" she asked.

Chapter 10

On Sunday morning, most kids in my neighborhood go to church. Usually, I do, too. But this Sunday, I was hunkered down in my mother's closet, breaking into her safe.

Now that I had become a professional liar, it hadn't taken much effort to fake sick and get out of going to church. I ate about five wintergreen LifeSavers, which makes your temperature go up for a few minutes. I call it Wintergreen Fever. (How I discovered that is another story entirely.) The trick is to not breathe too close to your mother, or she'll wonder why you have such great breath when you're sick.

I didn't have time to go to church. I needed to get some money, and quick. Sister Lucille could go into the treasury any day now to check the ledger card and see if it was time for us to make a deposit at the bank.

After I left Aurora's yesterday afternoon, I started with my Four-Part Plan to Get Out of This Bad Mess. Plan A was to raise as much money as I could as fast as I could in case I couldn't catch the real thief, which was Plan B. Plan C was pure and simple confession. I'd tell them I had done it. If I told them Maxey did it, she'd kill me, so saying I did it would save my life. Plan D was to go see if I could get a job at the Guatemalan missions until I did so much good everyone would just forgive me.

For the rest of the afternoon, I went door-to-door in the neighborhood next to mine, where I knew there were a lot of older people who needed help with some things that kids are good at. I used to help Grandpa with stuff all the time. I sat down on the curb and made up a flyer with the special pens I'd taken to Aurora's. Then I made thirty copies at the grocery store.

HARDWORKING DUTCH GIRL NEEDS WORK
"No job is too hard for me."
I have experience in cleaning kitty litter boxes, threading needles, testing for sour milk, picking fruit on high branches, opening safety caps, reading really small print (like expiration dates and the *TV Guide*), and sweeping garages.
I can also program a VCR and show you how to use the Internet to find out what happened on your soap if you missed it.
(I can understand English but do not speak it.)

By dinnertime on Saturday, I had earned $7.85 and had drunk four cups of tea, two glasses of juice, and one flat Coke from a very dusty glass. Old people are very worried about kids getting enough to drink. I had a couple of jobs set up for after school next week, but there was no way I was going to raise enough money from old people.

Which is why I was breaking into Mom's safe on God's Holy Day of Rest. I am pretty sure you get a double penalty for any sins you commit when you should be at church.

I'm not supposed to know the combination, but I do. I sort of accidentally memorized it one time when Mom opened the safe to get my savings book. I really tried to forget it but I never did.

The closet door squeaked as I pulled it open. I shoved away the big box of books that Mom puts in front of the safe to hide it, and scrunched down on my stomach. Cracking my knuckles, I spun the dial like they do in the movies.

Right spin to 12. Left one and a half spins to 33. Right to 39. Left back to 0.

I held my breath until the latch lifted. Easy and sweet. I reached deep into the safe and pulled out the Muriel cigar box. It was heavy like I remember. I didn't need to read the letter on top because I remembered every word of it.

But today I didn't want to remember what it said.

I didn't want to remember that Grandpa said he had been collecting these mint-condition silver dollars since he was a boy. And that if we hung on to them, they would be worth a lot someday. They're real silver through and through, and they've never been touched. Each one has its own special case. Half are mine and half are Maxey's.

I took eighty out and stuffed them into the bag I

brought from the kitchen. It was probably more than I needed, but I didn't know for sure. I'd never been to a pawnshop before.

But my dad had. Just once. And it changed his life forever.

• • •

With the address for Honest Abe's Pawnshop shoved deep in my pocket, I pedaled out of my neighborhood fast as I could go before anyone could see me. Not that they'd recognize me anyway. I was wearing a hooded sweatshirt and Maxey's sunglasses for a disguise.

It was a stroke of luck that they were having a pancake breakfast after church, so Mom and Maxey wouldn't be home until noon or so. Mom always liked to stay for cleanup, no matter what. It was one of those things about her that you could count on.

I wished she could help me clean up this mess. She probably could, but I didn't think I could survive her disappointment when she found out I let Maxey get the treasury keys from me.

Or that Maxey had taken the treasury money—maybe twenty, maybe eighty-seven dollars. I didn't know how, but I was going to have to wring the truth from her. I had to fix this real quick and hope to God Mom never, ever found out.

If Aurora and I had been established best friends, I could have turned to her to help me with this. But our friendship was too new.

HG's face popped up in my head. Wonder what she'd do in the same situation. Probably find something in her Bible to solve it. Every now and then I'd find a Bible verse on a tiny piece of folded-up paper in my desk. Like one of the times some mean kids were teasing me about my dad—later that afternoon I got a verse in my desk that said, "He prepareth a table before thee in the face of thine enemies." Which, after I read it a few times, I figured out meant that God will fix you dinner right in front of mean kids—I guess to make them jealous.

I'd rather he turn them all into warty toads. Be easier than trying to sit and eat while kids are picking on you. Even if it was the world's greatest dinner, fixed by God and everything.

I started to notice that the streets of Tyler Wash began to look very different. No more houses. Just lots of liquor stores and old hotels. My legs were tired from pedaling, and my shoulders ached from the weight of the eighty silver dollars in my backpack. Felt more like two hundred and eighty.

Honest Abe's Pawnshop was in the section of our city called Tiger Town. I don't know why they called it that, but I did know that I was not supposed to ever be riding my bike there.

It was easy to find. It was the only business on West Main Street that had a giant figure of President Lincoln in the window. At least Honest Abe's was honest in their ad in the phone book. It was open seven days a week. Even on a Sunday morning.

I parked my bike in front and locked it up tight. I studied the window display, which looked like a giant robbery heist. Lots of shiny things, electronic stuff, a few musical instruments, and a flesh-colored fake leg with a shoe still attached to it. I wondered what kind of trouble that poor person had gotten into that they'd had to sell their artificial leg.

"Hey, girrllll, got some change?" came a raspy voice from behind me.

I whirled around, my heart banging against my ribs. An old man stared at me with crusty eyes. His hand shook while he held it out to me. I wasn't usually scared of street people since Mom, me, and Maxey sometimes help out at the soup kitchen and I know a lot of them. But I was feeling pretty edgy today.

"I haven't eaten," he said with bad beer breath.

I dug into my backpack, past the silver coins, and pulled out a chocolate banana Endurance Bar. My mom bought them by the case. "Here," I said. "This will fill you up." I kept digging. "I have a mocha one, too," I said. "Eat both of these and you'll be set for hours."

He shoved them both into his coat pocket and stuck his hand out again. "Got some change, girl?" He moved a step closer to me. He didn't look dangerous, but his breath was close to doing me in. I wondered if he was someone's grandfather. I pulled a crumpled dollar out of my front pocket and handed it to him. I know you're not supposed to give money to people that drink, but maybe he'd buy some milk to go with the Endurance Bars. Just maybe.

He snatched the money from me, and he and my buck disappeared like some magic trick. Poof—gone!

I decided I'd better get off the street before I had any more visitors. The handle of the door to Honest Abe's was sticky with something creepy. I wiped my hands off on the seat of my pants as I walked in.

"Wanna pa-a-a-wn it? Wanna pa-a-a-wn it?" shrieked a terrible little voice as the door banged behind me.

I jumped. I didn't think my heart could handle much more of Tiger Town.

"Shut up, Kaufman!" A woman with giant blond hair came through an orange beaded curtain from the back. She coughed deeply from the bottom of her lungs and sort of smiled at me. "It's okay. It's just Abe's dumb bird," she said, cocking her head toward a dirty cage behind the counter.

Kaufman was a black bird with the darkest eyes I'd ever seen. He shrilled in that spooky voice that birds have, "We're buying, we're buying!"

The woman propped her elbows on the counter and gave me a long look. "So what can I do for you, Dorothy?"

"Dorothy?" I said, confused. "Uh, my name's Effeline." I put my hand across the counter. "Pleased to meet you, ma'am."

She shook my hand and laughed, which sent her into another fit of coughing. " 'S nice to meet you, Effeline. But you look like Dorothy who just wandered in from Kansas."

"Oh," I said, getting the joke and trying to smile. But my lips felt like someone had just smeared cement over them.

I cleared my throat and threw my backpack onto the

counter. "I have some silver dollars to sell." I pulled out my bag and shoved it over to her.

Pulling out a piece of felt, she smoothed it over the glass countertop, then spilled Grandpa's dollars over the top of it. She fingered a few gently, sort of respectful-like. "How old are you, Dorothy?"

"Fourteen . . . almost," I said with a dry swallow. Well, in just four more years.

"Tell you what. I am interested in buying these from you. Give you a good deal on them, too."

Kaufman whistled and flapped his wings. "Go-o-o-d deals here. Best price! Best price!" He sounded like he had a tiny salesman trapped inside him.

"How much?" I asked, trying to wet my lips with my tongue, which felt thick and stupid.

"How many you got here total?" she asked.

"Eighty," I said.

She nodded. "Okay, then, Dorothy. I'll take the whole collection for eighty big ones," she said. She patted her hair, which looked stiff enough to balance a load of bricks.

"You mean you'll give me eighty *hundred*—I mean, uh—" I broke off, trying to do the math quick. I knew "big ones" had to mean hundred-dollar bills. "I mean you'll give me eight thousand dollars?" I said, trying to sound cool and calm and not all gaspy like I felt.

She threw her head back and laughed, the whole front of her shaking—from the top of her boobs to her belly. "Eight thousand!" she croaked. "That's a good one!"

I felt my face start to burn with confusion.

She wiped at her eyes with one hand and dug through the tight space between her boobs. She fished out an old crumply tissue. "Honey! Not eight thousand. I'll give you *eighty* dollars."

"Eighty dollars! But there's eighty silver ones here! If I turned them in to the bank, I could get at least that!"

"So why don't you take them to the bank?" she asked.

I sighed. Naomi's mother worked at the bank. I couldn't exactly go waltzing in there with Grandpa's inheritance and try to exchange the coins. Somebody was bound to call my mother.

"Look," I said, trying to keep my voice even. "I'll take your eighty dollars, but that only buys forty of them. And that's my final offer," I said, folding my arms across my chest.

"Final offer! Final offer!" Kaufman shrieked.

She raised a long penciled eyebrow and began putting the dollars back into their bag.

I looked at her, frantic. "Eighty bucks for fifty of them, then!"

"Aw, honey, I was just yanking your chain. I can't buy these from you."

"Why not?" I asked, my voice up on the la-ti-do end of the music scale. "They're mine! I can show you the letter from my grandpa to prove it." For someone with as many lies as I had going, I felt very indignant that she didn't believe me.

Mrs. Honest Abe patted me on the shoulder. "I believe you, sugar. I just don't believe that your grandpa would approve of you selling them to me. If you want to prove me wrong, bring Grandpa with you. Then we'll talk."

Bring Grandpa. Yeah, right, I thought. I pictured bringing my thermos full of ashes and explaining that to her. I tried to suck in a deep breath.

She came around the corner, then, put a beefy arm around me. And handed me my sack. "You get on back to Kansas, little one. Go on, scoot."

"We'll buy any-thi-i-ing, just ask! Just ask!" Kaufman shouted.

I looked back over at his cage. And noticed the small sign tacked above it that read, GOOD IDEAS ARE PRICELESS.

Slinging my backpack over my shoulder, I just hoped I could come up with one real, real soon.

Chapter 11

I rolled three packs of wintergreen LifeSavers up on the counter at our local Stop'n Rob.

It was time to get some supplies for Monday morning's fever. And maybe Tuesday's fever, too. I was ready to move on to Plan B, and I needed some time off to think. I'd just played out all my Plan A cards.

I dug around in my front pockets for my money. The clerk watched me, chewing on a big old wad of chewing tobacco. He looked like a chipmunk storing nuts for the winter. He turned his head and spit into an old can on the floor.

"Hi, Effie," said a small voice that sounded like it came out of the floor.

Startled, I turned. HG stood behind me in line. She had an enormous cross around her neck and had a magazine rolled and tucked under one arm.

"Hey, hi!" I said.

Great, I thought. Just who I want to see in the middle of a crime spree—the most religious kid I know. I turned my front pants pockets inside out. Nothing but lint. I must have given the old guy in front of Honest Abe's my last dollar bill.

I gave Mr. Chew a quick grin. "Sorry, I know I've got money here somewhere." I nodded in HG's direction. "You go first. I'm not ready yet."

"Thanks," she said, moving up to the counter. "You duck out on the pancake breakfast, too?" she asked.

"Uh, yeah, s-sort of," I stammered. "I was home sick. Mom and Maxey went, though. But, I had to come get some more, um, well—LifeSavers."

She looked at my wintergreens and her eyes got big for a second. Then she nodded.

I flushed. "Well, I mean, uh, they help settle my stomach."

"Right," she said, her voice almost a whisper. HG grabbed her change off the counter and moved away.

The clerk looked over at me. "You buyin' these Life-Savers or not, kid?"

I dug through the bottom of my backpack, looking for loose change. Nothing but sunflower seed shells and three sticky pennies. A line of customers snaked behind me. Some helpful person cleared his throat, in case I hadn't noticed I was holding everybody up. My fingers closed around a coin inside its special case. I was out of options. I laid it up on the counter.

"Wow, a 1912 silver dollar!" The clerk guy had Grandpa's silver dollar held up between two fingers. He tried to whistle and dribbled brown juice down his chin. "Where'd you get this, kid?"

"My backpack," I said, exasperated. "Can I please just have my LifeSavers?"

HG's hand shot across the counter and grabbed the coin from him. She handed it back to me.

"Hey, what ya doing, girl?" he said.

She laid down a crumpled green bill. "It's my turn to buy the LifeSavers," she explained. She looked over at me, "Remember, Effie? You bought them last time." She held her hand out for the change.

Dazed, I just nodded.

She linked her arm with mine, scooped the LifeSavers up, and led me out of the store.

"Uh, thanks, HG—I mean *Trinity*," I said as she unlocked her bike. "You didn't have to do that, though."

"'S'kay," she said. "Didn't want that jerk to have your silver dollar." She fumbled with the lock, dropping her magazine. I reached over to pick it up for her. She leaned over and tried to grab it first. Our heads clunked hard.

"Ooouuch!" We both came up rubbing our heads. "Sorry!" we said in chorus. Which made us laugh for a second. And then it got silent because we didn't know what else to say.

She shoved her magazine under her arm, but not before I noticed the big vampire with bloody teeth on the front cover.

"Well, thanks again," I said, rubbing my forehead. Felt like it was starting to swell. "I could pay you back at school," I said.

"Forget it," she said. Her cheeks got red, and she cleared her throat. "Effie, I know about the Scout money," she said.

I threaded my arms through my backpack and tried to look casual. My heart was going crazy, though. "What ya mean?"

"I *mean* I know that Maxey and Phil got the treasury keys from you."

I chewed the inside of my cheek hard.

"You should tell on them, Effie," she whispered.

"I can't," I said, my voice flat.

She studied me a long second. Kind of creeped me out, like she was reading my mind. That was the thing about HG. She was an okay girl, but what my mom called *fey*. Like she could see things no one else could. I remember once in second grade when the bus driver couldn't find the bus keys. HG told him to go look on top of the fridge in the staff lunchroom.

Which was *exactly* where they were.

Another time this first grader disappeared during recess. Everyone was freaking out and calling the police. HG went into the old principal's office and told her to go check at Old Lady Gilhooley's house. Sure enough, that's where the kid was, sitting at the table having a snack. After that, everyone started treating HG like she was some kind of freak mind reader/fortune-teller. That's when she kind of closed up and climbed inside herself.

"So have you seen the pictures they bought with the money?" she asked, putting on her bike helmet.

"Pictures?" I said. "What pictures? Maxey said she paid a library fine."

She shook her head. "Marcus Crenshaw took some pictures of Mr. Constantino. Then he took some pictures of

Maxey. Put the photos together on the computer so they look like a couple. Maxey bought the disk from him."

I stared at her, incredulous. "*That's* what she spent the money on?"

"Some of it," HG said.

"Do you know how much she took out?" I asked, half afraid to hear the answer.

"I know they were planning to take twenty, but they bought some other stuff, so I'm not really sure," she said.

"What other stuff?" I asked, moving way past mad.

HG stuffed her magazine in the pack on her bike. "They bought some new earrings and a tiger skin headband for Maxey to wear in the picture, but then Phil gets to keep the stuff. Maxey just wants the disk."

A dusty jeep roared up in front of us. Shouting boys of all sizes poured out, racing each other through the front door. As the cloud settled, Aurora Triboni jumped from the jeep, Bradley stuck to her hip. Mr. Triboni stayed in the car and turned the music to a cowboy station.

"Hi, Ef," she called as she came toward us. "Hey, HG. What are you two doing here?" she asked, emphasis on the "you two."

We both stammered, tongue-tied, like we'd been caught at something.

Aurora looked amused and a little puzzled. "That's some cross, HG. Does Father McCabe know you borrowed the church steeple?" she asked with a grin.

I managed a weak little laugh.

HG pulled her bike lock off and hurried to leave.

"Aw, come on. Don't go off in a huff. I was just teasing. It's pretty, really."

Bradley drilled the hole in his nose with his finger. Aurora flushed and tried to brush his hand away. "Gawd. I hate when he does that."

"Oh, Effie," she said. "I finished my part of the report for our Discovery Project. Found some good stuff on the Internet about the history of you-know-what," she said with a glance at HG.

HG buckled her helmet and mumbled a quick good-bye. She bumped her bike down the curb.

Aurora shouted after her, "Hey, don't be mad about the cross thing. I'm sorry!"

See, this is what I liked about Aurora. She would never hurt anybody on purpose—not like Maxey or Kayla. HG was just being supersensitive like always.

"I didn't know you guys were friends," Aurora said, watching HG ride off. She shrugged and turned back to look at me.

"I don't hang out with her," I said quickly. "Our sisters are best friends, so I kind of know her that way. She's an okay kid." I rammed my hands into my pockets and felt my cheeks grow red. "I don't really have a best friend anymore. Not since Lola Jo moved away."

Aurora studied me a moment and then looked away. "Yeah, me neither."

The silence between us got thick as honey. This was one of those life-changing moments. But one of us needed to make the first move.

"Aurora, um, do you wanna—" I began.

"Well, maybe we—" she started at the same time.

We both laughed and said, "You go first."

Aurora wiped her bangs out of her eyes and hitched Bradley up a notch on her hip.

"Look, Ef, here's the thing. I really would like to have a new best friend—and you're great—really nice and funny—but Kayla, well, she's really bugging me to make up with her. I keep telling her she and I are *capital Q* Quits, but she keeps calling me and asking me to do stuff with her. She's kind of hard to say no to."

Bradley squealed and tried to shinny down Aurora's leg as the Triboni brothers came out of the store. They had giant sodas and bags of chips the size of pillows. Aurora and Bradley were sucked back into their noisy ranks and lifted into the jeep.

"Gotta go—we can talk more about it later. See ya tomorrow, Effie!" Aurora yelled as the jeep peeled out of the parking lot.

I waved and smiled back, long and hard. And stood there in the parking lot still waving until my hand almost fell off and my teeth dried up. Because when she turned back around to wave one last goodbye, I wanted her to see what a loyal, devoted, stick-to-your-side best friend I could be.

But she forgot to turn around.

Chapter 12

Even though I'd stayed home sick from church and the pancake breakfast and had to lie in bed all Sunday afternoon, there was no way Mom was going to cancel our weekly Team Meeting that we had every Sunday night. It used to be called Family Night, at least that's what Maxey says, until Dad left and Mom went back to work as a coach and our whole world turned into a giant sports game. Grandpa said it was the only way Mom could make her life make sense. There were rules for everything, and everyone knew what they were supposed to do, and you got points if you did it just right. And if you got fouled, there was a big loud noise about it and they had to make it up to you somehow right on the spot.

We did all kinds of stuff at our Team Meetings. We'd usually eat first, then sometimes Mom would have us help her pay the bills to teach us to be "financially independent" when we grew up. Sometimes she'd put an exercise tape in the VCR and we'd work out together, but Maxey only liked the exercises for a tight butt. One night Mom taught us how to make spaghetti from scratch. Last Sunday, we cleaned out a closet and gave some extra clothes to the poor.

But the one thing we never did at our Sunday-night meeting was talk about Dad, and we hardly even talked about Grandpa anymore. It was like Mom had a very short memory for men who left her.

I squirted a long straight line of catsup on a single french fry, careful not to squiggle.

"Mom!" Maxey whined from across the coffee table. "Effie is totally hogging the catsup again!"

Mom looked up from the *Financial Times* magazine she was reading. I could tell we were going to get another money talk tonight after we finished eating. "Ef, give your sister the catsup when you're done," she said.

I handed it over and popped the fry into my mouth. We didn't get take-out hamburgers and fries too often because Mom said they were cheaper to make, and I wanted to savor each and every bite. "Mmm. These are so good, Mom."

Maxey squirted a big pool of catsup on the edge of her plate. As soon as she set it down, I reached for it again and laid another careful red line down a fry.

Maxey looked over at me, her eyes getting squinty. "Mom! She's doing it again!"

Mom reached for her glasses and turned the page. "Girls, settle down and eat your dinners."

"Do you really need this back?" I asked. "You already put some on your plate."

"Yes, I need it," she said. She pulled the top bun off her burger and flipped it on its back.

She made several quick lines and loops across her bun, and then what looked like an exclamation point. She turned the bun around so it was facing me. It read

freak!

"May I please have the catsup for my fries?" I asked, pretending not to read her bun.

"Sure!" she said, leaning over and squeezing a giant splatty load of catsup all over my plate.

"Mo-o-om!" I cried. "Look what Maxey did!"

Mom threw her magazine down and pulled off her glasses. "Maxine! What do you think you're doing?"

"I was just trying to be helpful—she said she needed some catsup." Maxey slapped her bun back on top of the burger to hide any evidence.

Mom looked at our plates, then switched them around, giving Maxey my plate with the catsup disaster on it.

Maxey looked horrified. "I'm not eating off her plate. She never washes her hands after she pees."

"I do too wash my hands!" I cried. "And I'm not eating her burger, Mom. And she knows why!" I said, glaring at her.

"TIME OUT!" Mom called, stabbing her fingertips in the palm of her other hand like the referees on TV do. "You two have about fifteen seconds to start eating some-body's burger, or you both are going to spend the rest of the night in your room." She gave us a hard look and set the timer on the big giant coach watch she wore even on the weekends.

"I mean it!" she said. "Fourteen, thirteen, twelve—"

Maxey put her elbows on the coffee table and just stared at me. I knew she'd wait until the very last second before she'd do what Mom told her.

"El-e-ven, ten, nine, eight," Mom ticked away.

I grabbed my burger back from Maxey and took a big bite. She studied her fingernails.

"Seven, Maxey, six—*five*—four," Mom said, her voice hard.

Maxey's eyes drilled into mine. "I'm not eating anything that the FREAK breathed on."

And, then, I don't know what came over me. I was so tired of her picking on me and making my life miserable. I grabbed her burger and took a big sloppy bite out of hers, too. Then I shoved the plate toward her.

Maxey screamed and came over the top of the coffee table at me, knocking me and all the sodas to the floor. She grabbed my hair and the front of my shirt and everything else she could get her hands on and shook me like an old rag doll. I was too stunned to do anything.

"Max-ine!" Mom yelled, jumping to her feet. She crouched over and pulled Maxey off me. She threw her over on the end of the sofa and pointed a sharp finger at Maxey's nose. "You stay right there, young lady!"

Mom pulled me out from where I was stuck between the sofa and coffee table. My shirt was all wet from the spilt sodas. She ripped off my shirt. I crossed my arms over my boobs, feeling very naked. I was too old for even my mother to be looking.

"Are you all right, Ef?" Mom asked, giving me a quick once-over.

I shrugged and rubbed the back of my head where it had hit the floor. "I . . . uh . . . guess so," I said, watching the little yellow canary that was flying circles around my head.

"Here," Mom said, handing me my wadded-up shirt. "Go put this in the washer and grab one of the team shirts off the top of the dryer. Then come right back here."

I kinda walked-staggered to the laundry room, and by the time I got there, I was boiling mad. I hated Maxey! The devil himself wouldn't want her for a sister. I kicked the washing machine a good one before I dropped my shirt inside. I grabbed St. Ignacio's number 11 off the dryer and pulled it over me. It came to my knees, but it was dry.

I was telling! I was going to go out there and tell Mom everything. Mom needed to know that not only was Maxey a big fat bully, she was a good-for-nothing crook, just like—

"Effie! Let's go!" Mom hollered at me from the other room. "Did you find a dry shirt?"

"Coming!" I yelled. And Maxey just better look out. Mom was probably going to be so mad she'd send Maxey to one of those special reform schools where they send really bad girls.

Mom pointed to Grandpa's old recliner next to the sofa, where Maxey sat looking pale but still really mad.

"Sit," Mom said. She sat forward, elbows on her knees, and squeezed the skin between her eyes. I could tell she was squeezing it very hard. "Maxey, apologize to your sister, and 'I'm sorry' are the only two words I want to hear out of your mouth."

"Sorry," Maxey mumbled.

"Effie, I want you to apologize for your part in all this."

"But, Mo-o-m—" I started.

"NOW!" she shouted, and I could see there was no point in arguing with her.

"I'm sorry," I said, and wondered if God would count this as a sin because it was a total lie that I was sorry for anything.

"I've just had it with the two of you," Mom yelled, her voice getting all shaky at the end. "I cannot do this all by myself!" She slammed back on the couch and grabbed at her hair like she was going to pull it out by the roots.

Maxey and I looked at each other a second. We'd heard Mom say that before, but never quite like this. Like she really couldn't take us anymore. I gulped. "We're sorry, Mom. We'll try harder."

Maxey scooted a little closer to her on the sofa. "And if Effie promises to behave better, Mom, I won't be so tempted to hit her all the time."

"I have to get another job, girls," Mom blurted. "We're just not making it. It's either that or take you out of private school, and I just don't want to do that."

"What kind of job?" I asked, digging my teeth into my lip.

"I can do some extra coaching over at the public high school in the evenings and on the weekends."

"Public school!" Maxey said, horrified. "Why would you want to coach those kids?"

Mom gave us both a long look. "This was one of the things I wanted to talk to you both about tonight. About whether I could trust you two to stay home alone together. I can't really afford to hire a babysitter for you."

"We don't need a babysitter, Mom!" Maxey said. "I'm almost thirteen! I can handle Effie."

"Right! I saw how you 'handled' Effie tonight. I just can't leave the two of you home alone—and since I don't want to spend all the extra money I'm earning on babysitters, I'm going to take Sister Clementia up on her offer."

"What offer?" I asked.

"Well, when I talked to her about taking on some extra work after school a while back, she said you girls could come over to the convent in the evenings and do your homework."

"No way!" Maxey said, her face going as white as her hair. "Mom! You can't do this to me. The kids will laugh me right out of school!"

"Maxey," Mom said with a deep sigh, "your friends will never know. And when you're there on the weekends—"

"WEEKends!" Maxey and I yelled.

"I'm going to have to work some weekend games from time to time. You can help the Sisters clean the church and the classrooms. Sister Lucille offered to pay you each a dollar an hour, but I told her that wouldn't be necessary, since they'll be doing us a huge favor."

Maxey slumped down in her seat, and I raked my teeth back and forth over my bottom lip. Maxey was right. If the kids found out, and they would, we'd never hear the end of it. They'd probably start calling us Sister Maxey and Sister Effie and we'd start finding rosary beads in our desks and I'd never learn any of the good cuss words that you learn in fifth grade. Look what happened to HG, and all she did was read the Bible.

"Effie, stop scraping your lip," Mom said.

Maxey bit the head off a bloody french fry. "Philomena Finch says all the nuns at St. Dominic's are lezzies. What if one of them tries to kiss me? I'll just die—"

"*What* have I told you about lesbians, Maxine?" Mom cut in, her voice exasperated.

Maxey dropped her chin. "Sorry—they're very smart ladies and we shouldn't say mean things about them ever."

Mom sighed and continued. "Look, girls, I'm sorry. I know that it doesn't seem like much of a solution to you, but it's the only way. I hate that I have to take a second job, but we've almost gone through all our savings, and our car is on its last legs. I just pray each day we don't have any kind of unexpected financial emergency. I don't know what I'd do."

My heart took a long slow walk out on a plank and dove, headfirst—landing with a big, splashy, painful thud.

Chapter 13

"You're faking." Maxey stood over me, her eyes narrowed. "And you were faking yesterday, I bet."

Mom came out of the bathroom shaking out the thermometer.

"Maxey, get ready for school and leave your sister alone. Do you really want to lose your first success star this early in the day?" She came over and laid her cheek on my forehead again.

I held in my very fresh breath. I'd eaten about six wintergreens this time, just to be extra sure.

"Well, kiddo, you don't feel warm, but you're still running a little high. Same as yesterday. Your head still hurt?" She brushed my hair off my forehead.

I shut my eyes and nodded. And that was no lie. I'd given myself an Olympic-sized headache from worrying. I'd spent all day yesterday afternoon on the Internet coming up with a list of things I could do to earn some quick cash. I came up with sixty-two ways. You had to have a college degree for thirty-six of them, and for three of the ways you needed to speak a foreign language. You needed a car for twelve of the jobs, and I'd need Mom's permission for most of the rest of them.

Now I had a list of sixty-one things crossed out and one left. Number sixty-two was calling my dad and asking him to loan me some money. But I don't think he has any money where he's at, and if he does, he can't get it to me by tomorrow probably.

My last hope was the Booger Boy himself.

Maxey sat down hard on my bed, on the place that squeaks. "I don't feel good either, Mom. Maybe I should stay home. I think I might be getting the Cramps."

Mom looked over at her. "Max, I think we've got at least another year before you start your period. And when you do, 'the Cramps' will not be a reason to stay home from school, or an excuse to get out of gym class, ever."

Maxey glared at me. "You better not touch any of my stuff while I'm at school today, Effie. Don't even look at my side of the room." She flounced over to her closet to grab a sweater.

"Maxey," Mom said, as she started out the door, "before you leave the house, please go into the bathroom and take out whatever it is you have stuffed in your bra."

Maxey stopped dead in her tracks and whirled around, arms crossed over her chest. "I don't have anything stuffed—"

"You're lopsided," Mom sighed. "Out with it, missy."

The bathroom door banged with a vengeance.

Mom straightened the covers over me. "Let's keep you

home one more day just to be safe. Same drill as yesterday, rest and fluids." She checked her watch. "I'll go call the school, then I'll pop across the street and see if Mrs. Korn can come by again today and check on you. You've got my beeper number, and if you start feeling worse, you call me. And I'll be home to fix you lunch, okay?"

I nodded, hoping she'd lean down and kiss me like she used to. Instead, she checked her watch and then made sure I had the barf bucket nearby.

I waited awhile until I heard the front door bang and knew that Maxey had left for school. Then I waited until I heard Mom turn on the downstairs shower. Even still, I crept on my tiptoes over to our computer in the corner of our bedroom. It was one of those big old-fashioned kind. Mom had bought it for us at the high school when they were getting rid of their old computers.

I hefted the monitor up and to the side, then pried open the lid on the hard drive. It was big and roomy inside. Lot of wasted space. Perfect for hiding something you never, ever want anyone to find.

Like someone's ashes.

I snuck back to bed with my thermos full of Grandpa and pulled the blankets over my head. And snaked a hand out to grab my flashlight from my nightstand. I lit up my little undercover cave. Unscrewing the cap on my thermos, and careful not to spill, I peeked inside. I'm not sure what I was looking for, but I always had to take a quick look. I took a long sniff. He didn't smell like himself anymore, but it was still him in there.

"Hey, Grandpa," I whispered. I screwed the cap back,

but never too tight. Grandpa hated things that were too tight. He was always loosening his necktie. I flipped over onto my side, and I held him close to me.

If he were still alive, he'd know right away something was wrong. He could read me like a book, he'd always say. And I wasn't any mystery, he'd add, laughing and rubbing the back of my neck. When he thought I had something on my mind, he'd take me out for a long walk, not saying much and not prying, either. But before I knew it, I'd be spilling my guts all over the sidewalk. I still couldn't believe he wasn't here anymore. Even after a year, it still squeezed me bad inside.

Getting over Dad wasn't so hard. I was too young to remember him, really. I had just turned four and Maxey was almost six when it all happened. Mostly what I knew about him was from Maxey or stories I'd heard about him from the older kids. Stories that made me feel ashamed, even though Mom always told us that what he did had nothing to do with us.

It was harder on Maxey. She remembered Dad and really missed him a lot. I think that's why she was so stuck on Mr. Constantino. She thought she was in love with him. I think it was just her way of missing Dad.

Grandpa never talked too much about Dad either. Mom said that was because he missed him so much. I asked Mom if she missed Dad, and she always said that he left the best of himself in me and Maxey and that was all she needed. I wondered if that was her way of not talking about it.

Seemed like there was an awful lot of people missing people in my family and not saying too much about it. I swallowed around the small hot rock that lived in the back of my throat. The one that kept me from talking about it.

• • •

Hours later, I found the number I needed from the telephone book and looked up at the clock. It was four on the nose. School had been out for thirty minutes. He should be home by now.

Punching in the telephone numbers, I took a deep breath. I closed the door to Mom's office with my big toe. The smell of something chocolate and delicious came sneaking in from under the door. Mom was baking my favorite, frosted hazelnut brownies. She was probably trying to lure me back to health. My mouth grew warm and wet, and I almost slobbered right onto the carpet.

I wiped the sweat off my forehead. This whole mess was giving me a real fever. "Uh, hello, Mrs. Crenshaw? Is Marcus home? This is Maxine Maloney," I lied.

"Hey, Maxey, how ya doing?" Marcus's familiar voice came on the line after a minute, making my skin crawl.

I cleared my throat again and pulled out my best fake Maxey voice. "Marcus, I want my money back."

"No way," he said, his voice cheerful. "We had a deal. Besides, you got the disk."

"I don't want the disk. You can have it back. I haven't even looked at it."

"No thanks. I'll just keep the money. You keep the disk."

"Lookit, Crenshaw," I said, my voice getting mad and shrill, "that money wasn't even mine to spend. I stole it from my poor little sister. And she is in a bunch of trouble now. We've got to help her out."

Marcus paused a moment and then laughed. "Effie, is that you? This has got to be you, right?" He snorted, then laughed again. "You gave yourself away. Like Maxey would care if she got you in trouble."

"Marcus, I need that money back. If you don't, I'm going to tell Ms. Obermeyer on you!" I threatened.

"For what? Taking Mr. Constantino's picture? That's no crime." His voice got quiet then, and sneaky sweet. "Look, kid. I don't give refunds. It's bad for business. But I'm always open for a new deal. You got something you could sell, maybe?"

I thought about the baby picture of Maxey grinning from the seat of her Twinkle Twinkle Little Star potty. I wouldn't mind that getting around school.

He went on, his voice getting more sinister by the moment. "Just so happens I'm having my own little science fair before assembly tomorrow. I'm calling it 'Marc's Amazing Marvels and Gross-outs.' I'm in the market for some new stuff."

My palms were clammy, and I wiped them on the front of my bathrobe. "How about inventions?" I asked, hopeful. "I have the world's greatest Discovery Project." I tried to imagine explaining to Aurora why I had sold our Discovery Project before we even showed it to the class.

"Nah, that's kid stuff. I'm talking *real* marvels. So far, I've got my booger collection, an infected tooth, and a giant earwax ball. A fifth grader is bringing me a dead two-headed snake, and I got a pair of gym socks from the junior varsity football team. They stink so bad they'll make your eyes water. Buzz says they had a contest to see how many kids could wear them without ever washing them. I paid ten bucks for those babies," he announced proudly. "And one of my big toenails is two inches long now. It's really something to see!" He lowered his voice. "But you haven't heard the best yet."

I couldn't wait to hear what was coming.

"Billy Martindale's mother is, you know, uh, 'bra feeding' Billy's new baby sister. Billy is going to bring me some of her real live milk. Says his mom pumps it out and has tons of it in the fridge. She'll never miss a little bit of it gone. How cool is that?"

"That's disgusting, Marcus."

"Yeah, and that's why it's so cool," he said with a happy sigh. "So, Ef, think you got anything? Any old body parts lying around, or maybe a big jar of toe jam? Hey! Maybe something gross from Maxey. The guys would love it!"

My heart skidded to a stop. I knew I had something better than any of that.

But I couldn't sell them, could I? Then I remembered Mom's face last night when she was talking about how broke we were and how she'd go right off the deep end if we had any money emergencies. I was pretty sure having to pay back the Scout treasury eighty-seven dollars would count as one of those emergencies.

I had to do it. "I've got something that will blow the roof off your whole show," I said. "But it's going to cost you big!"

"What is it?" he said, excited. I could feel him starting to pant on the other end of the line. Ick. Marcus was half boy, half slug.

"First off, it's gonna cost you to even hear what it is. Then it's gonna cost you plenty to see it and even more for you to show it to anyone. And I get it back or there's no deal. I'm not selling them, just renting them out for a while." Geez, like that was going to make my conscience or poor Grandpa feel any better.

"How much for you to tell me what it is?"

"Ten bucks," I said, all business.

"Just to hear what it is?" he said.

"Yep, that's the deal. But once you hear it, if you don't think it was worth it, you don't have to pay. But you'll totally think it's worth it. I guarantee it."

"Okay, what the heck," he laughed. "It's win-win for me."

I covered my mouth over the phone and whispered what it was.

Marcus sucked in his breath, then let out a long whistle. "Are you *serious*?" he asked.

"Scout's honor," I said, then wished I hadn't. Having lost the entire Scout treasury didn't leave me with any extra honor to throw around. This whole mess was my fault. If I hadn't let those stupid keys out of my sight in the first place, none of this would have happened.

"Okay, I'm ready to do business with you, kid. How much is it gonna cost me to show them?"

98

I did some quick math in my head. I needed at least eighty to go with the money I'd earned over the weekend. "Seventy bucks to show them, plus you owe me ten bucks for getting to hear what it was."

He exhaled hard into the phone. "You're asking for a lot of dough."

"Of course," I said, thinking fast on my feet, "I could just have my own show and cut you out. There's three hundred kids at St. Dominic's. If every kid paid me a dollar to see them—" I started.

"Hey, no need for that!" he said. "You're lucky you caught me feeling generous. Just so happens I've come into a wad of cash this week. Ef, you got yourself a deal."

I set the phone down and collapsed into Mom's chair, then wiped the sweat off my face with the front of my pajamas. I spun myself around slowly with one foot and thought about the "wad of cash" Marcus had mentioned. Maybe Maxey hadn't lied to me! Maybe Marcus had stolen the other sixty-seven dollars from the treasury. Or maybe he'd gotten all the money from Maxey. HG said Maxey and Phil were planning on taking twenty from the treasury, but maybe they had taken it all. I'm sure if Marcus had an old stinky sock from Mr. Constantino, Maxey would give him fifty bucks for it.

I needed to talk to somebody. I was in urgent need of another brain on this with me to sort it all out. Mom wouldn't let me call Lola Jo long distance, and writing a letter would take too long. Plus, as much as I hated to admit it, I didn't feel very close to her anymore. In her last letter, all she could talk about was the new girl who moved in next door and how they had the same birthday and the same freckle on the palms of their hands and "isn't that just so cool?"

I wished I could call Aurora. I'd have her come right over and rough up Maxey until she begged for mercy and spit the whole truth out. I spun the chair around faster and faster, imagining Aurora wearing a big scary hockey mask and some shoulder pads. She'd have on a sleeveless shirt and maybe she'd have grown even more black underarm hairs—she'd stand over Maxey and growl. And, then, after Maxey confessed everything and ran off to go hide under the bed for a couple of years, Aurora would tell me that she had a secret bank account that had exactly eighty-seven dollars in it, and since I was her new best friend, she'd let me borrow it for as long as it took me to pay it back.

I dialed Aurora's number. I'd been practicing so I knew it by heart. One of the big brothers answered with a very grouchy voice, so I hung right up.

HG's face popped into my head. She had a funny habit of doing that. Despite her weirdness, I kinda liked talking to her. There was something about her I'd been noticing lately that kinda drew me in. But being best friends with HG would put me on the Forever Weird list at school. Plus, I bet she'd just tell me again to tell Mom, and I wasn't going to do that. No way.

I had to handle this on my own without Mom knowing anything. I stood up and tightened my bathrobe tie around me, then tightened it again. Like it or not, I had just been magically cured of Wintergreen Fever. It was time to get back to school. It was showtime.

Chapter 14

I ate three frosted hazelnut brownies before I went to bed to make sure I'd be wide awake after Mom went to sleep at ten o'clock. Even though I'd been lying around a lot for three days, I was very tired. And I had to stay awake so I could sneak down into the garage, because that's where we kept the kitty litter and tiny aquarium rocks.

'Cause I'd decided right in the middle of dinner that there was no way I was going to show Grandpa's real ashes. And why should I have to? If I could fool my mom and Maxey, surely I could fool a bunch of dumb boys.

It was bad enough that I had to give up my Grandpa-in-a-thermos secret. I swear if any of those kids ever told on me, I was dead meat. But it was a chance I was just going to have to take. I was praying I'd be able to scare them into keeping the lid on this. I've noticed boys are kind of su-perstitious and respectful about scary things.

I waited until I heard Mom finish up in her bathroom and close her bedroom door. Then I waited another half hour to be sure she was asleep. She does fifty sit-ups and fifty push-ups before she gets into bed. Then she prays the rosary until she falls asleep.

Fortunately, the brownies were working. I was very awake. Plus, I'd put three pairs of socks on my feet as extra insurance. I can't ever fall asleep if my feet are hot. They were on fire. I was half expecting to see smoke coming out from under the covers.

At ten-thirty p.m., I took a peek at Maxey. She was dead to the world. Too bad she couldn't stay that way.

I grabbed my flashlight and slid out of bed. The extra socks made me especially sneaky. I tiptoed down the stairs, skipping over the step that always made a cracking noise when you put your foot on it.

As I crept through the kitchen I grabbed a plastic container from the dish drainer. It knocked a glass off, which rolled onto the counter and almost right onto the floor before I caught it. I froze and held my breath a second, hoping Mom wouldn't come tearing down the stairs with the tennis racket she keeps under her bed for bad guys. (Maxey keeps a bat for backup.)

Still quiet on the second floor. I let my breath out in relief.

The kitchen door to the garage made a tiny click as I opened it, but in the dark, it sounded like a giant clang. I closed the door ever so quietly behind me, but not all the way so it wouldn't click again.

The garage was freezing cold and a lot spookier than it looks in the daytime. I got this bad creepy feeling that there might be someone hiding in our Volkswagen who might pop out when I wasn't looking. I kept one eye on the car while I moved around it and shined the flashlight up against the side wall.

Right where the kitty litter used to be. Oh, no. This was not a good week for us to be out of litter.

I scooched past the gardening tools over to the closet where we keep extra supplies. I scanned the rows of laundry detergent, toilet paper, bottled water, charcoal, aquarium rocks. I dug open the bag and took a handful out and put them in my cup.

I held it up to my flashlight, then sighed real loud and poured them back into the bag. They were the bright blue kind. You can't have *blue* ashes. No one, not even boys, was dumb enough to fall for that.

I studied the empty container, thinking. Geez Louise. This was much easier last time. I ran the flashlight over the front wall, seeing what else I might find. Pretty Girl's litter box was on the floor in the corner. I moved over to it and squatted down in front of it. Guess I could just take a little of it. Might not smell too good, but boys like bad smells. Maybe it would make it seem more convincing. I scooped up a bit from what looked like the cleanest corner of the box. I could mix it up with some black pepper from the kitchen, then—

The overhead garage light flipped on, blinding me.

"Effie!" Mom said. "What are you *doing* out here?"

"Um—uh," I sputtered. I looked down at my plastic container. "I was cleaning out the litter box?"

Mom looked at me like I was six miles past crazy.

I hurried on. "I was lying in bed and remembered I hadn't done it for a couple of days, and you know how fussy Pretty Girl is." This was all sounding very lame, even to me.

"And you're using our good Tupperware to do it?" Mom took it out of my hand and dumped it back out. She put the container on the washing machine. "Come inside. It's freezing out here."

I let her lead me in while I finished working on my recipe in my head. I'd throw it together in the morning while she was in the shower.

One cup of slightly used kitty litter, one tin of pepper, and a handful of sand from the neighbor kid's sandbox—mix it all together.

It would work. It had to.

Mom felt my forehead as she sat me down on one of our kitchen counter stools. "You having a hard time sleeping?" she asked.

I nodded. Who wouldn't with a pound of chocolate sitting in their stomach and feet on fire?

"Let's fix some herbal tea to help you relax, huh?" She turned on the little stove light, but not the big overhead light. Just like she used to do when I was little and she was trying to get me to fall back asleep. She'd fix me something warm to drink and talk to me in a real soft voice.

"Does this late-night prowling have anything to do with your Discovery Project?" she asked as she got our cups ready. "Everything going okay with that?"

"Oh, we're ready!" I said. That was actually the only

thing working in my life right now. "I finished my report on Sunday. And Aurora said she was going to make some more samples of our invention. Hey, do you think I could have her overnight this weekend? We're almost best friends already. It might be official by then."

"So you think you'll be well enough to go to school tomorrow?" Mom asked. Then she peered out the kitchen window "Though I almost hate to have you go out. A big storm is supposed to be moving in tonight."

"I *have* to go, Mom!" I said, aghast. "I can't let Aurora down."

She looked at me and smiled. "You're one true-blue kid, Effie. She'd be lucky to have you for a best friend."

I felt my face start to burn and I lowered my head. I was glad it was dark in the kitchen and Mom couldn't see my face. True blue I was not. I was that color you get when you mix too many colors.

Greenish brown.

I was a lousy treasurer, Maxey's personal stooge, a liar, and, as of tomorrow, I was adding cheat to my list. I'd be cheating every kid who was paying good money to see Grandpa's real ashes. And I was conning Marcus, which still was bad, even if he was a very disgusting boy.

But I just couldn't show a bunch of boys the real ashes. I knew it was very wrong, but I had very special circumstances. It had to be okay to cheat a few kids out of some measly bucks if it meant protecting your poor dead grandpa from being in a freak show. Wasn't it?

Mom slid a cup of tea over to me and I took a tiny sip. I

tried to sort out some of the stuff that was whipping around my head like a tornado.

"Mom?" I asked, trying to sound casual. "I was reading this book today about some very bad people—you know, for an extra-credit book report I might do for religion class. And I was wondering. Do you think there might ever be special circumstances where it's okay to cheat people— just a *little*—if they're not gonna know, and if you've got to do it to protect your family?"

She took a deep breath and shoved her hands into the pockets of her fuzzy green robe. "Ef, are you talking about your dad?" she asked.

I raised my shoulders, then dropped them, surprised.

"Effie, cheating is never okay, you know that. What Dad did was wrong, even if he convinced himself it was for us. It was never really about us, though. It was always about money. He wanted it to come easier than it did. All the dreams he thought he had for our family—those were his dreams, not mine, not ours."

I thought she wasn't going to say anything else because she got very quiet for a minute. But then she went on. "He really wasn't a bad man, Ef, but he was a very weak one."

"But then how did—?" I stopped, not sure how to ask.

"He let his partner take advantage of him. That was his downfall. He couldn't stand up to Ben. And, then, when he realized what they were into, it was just too late to stop it."

"And you *never* knew what was going on?" I asked.

She looked deep into her teacup. "Not until I found out he had pawned our wedding rings."

I'd heard this part before, but it still stunned me every time. The day Mom found out about the rings, she got my dad to confess the whole miserable mess he was in. Dad told her he and Mr. Hocker had "borrowed" a few million dollars from some clients to make some more money, and then somehow they'd lost all the money they borrowed. Dad had pawned their wedding rings just to make a quick payment on a loan from some crook. Mom told him to turn himself in to the police or she would.

"Don't you ever feel bad for making him turn himself in, Mom?" I asked, hoping maybe she did a little.

Mom shook her head. "No, it was the last right choice left in that whole sorry mess. If I regret anything, it's that I didn't see it coming. If only I could have done something, anything, to prevent all those poor people from being cheated out of their money," she said, her voice raggedy around the edges.

I took my cup over to the sink so I wouldn't have to look at her.

"I know it's been tough on you and Max," she said, coming up behind me and squeezing my shoulders kinda hard. "All we can do is keep our heads up and live honest, decent lives—be the kind of people that others can trust. That's how we love and protect in this family, Ef."

She gave me a big "go team" slap on the behind.

When you need a giant Mom-can-fix-anything hug, a slap on the butt just sort of leaves you cold. I left the room before I got the high five.

Chapter 15

When I woke up early Wednesday morning, my sheets were all untucked and nearly strangling me. Rain sprayed our bedroom window, and the wind banged a loose shutter. My head felt tight and achy. I would have sworn I hadn't slept a second, but I must have. All night that old bird from the pawnshop had been chasing me down. Like a little undertaker, all dressed in black, nearly licking his beak to get at me.

I rolled over and looked at Maxey, who was still asleep. She had one hand tucked under her face. She looked so different when her face was still and she wasn't making mean, squinty faces at me. I tried to imagine us ever being friends like Grandpa said we would. Tried to imagine her ever being the one who I would run to with my troubles.

Like the big trouble I was headed for today. The trouble that had Maxey's fingerprints all over it. That all started because of her dumb crush on Mr. Constantino. Well, she could have him as far as I was concerned. Hopefully, after today, I'd have Aurora Triboni as my new best friend. We'd tell each other everything. And I'd stop being Maxey's stooge for *good*.

I'd hoped Aurora would call me while I was home sick two days to see how I was doing. But she didn't.

She must have been very busy taking care of her brothers. HG called, though. I had Mom tell her I was too sick to talk. Mom gave me a Serious Look about that. Which made me feel very guilty, but I didn't want to tie up the phone just in case Aurora did get a break from doing a lot of chores. What if she wanted to call me up about our Discovery Project, or about staying overnight sometime, and I was yakking away on the phone with HG?

Maxey's clock radio blinked to 6:00 a.m. and the morning weather watch filled our room. Maxey reached over and bonked the top button down. One eye peered over in my direction, and she rubbed the other with a fist.

"You ever going back to school?" she asked, a yawn taking over her face.

"Today," I said, my voice tired as a ninety-year-old's.

"I don't know how you do it, but I know you've been faking your fever," she said. "You did the same thing last year when they were having the fitness tests at school. Philomena says HG can do it too. She says she bets HG pulls a fever today because she's supposed to do her Discovery Project and she doesn't even have a partner yet. That," Maxey said, "is one weird kid."

"She's not weird!" I said, feeling pretty steamed in

HG's defense. It was one thing for me to think that—but hearing Maxey say it really chapped my hide. "She's just different," I said. "Smart, nice, and different. Nothing wrong with that."

"So then how come you didn't ask her to be your Discovery Project partner?" Maxey asked. "How come you barely even ever talk to her at school, huh?"

"Shut up, Maxey," I said.

She reached under her mattress and pulled out a small wrinkled bag. She rooted around in it a minute. "Want some jelly beans?" she offered. She drew the bag back and raised her eyebrow. "Tell me how you fake a fever, and I'll give you the whole bag."

"I don't want any of your stale old jelly beans! I want all the treasury money back!"

Maxey sighed. "Is that all you can talk about anymore? I told you a hundred times I didn't take it! I just took twenty to pay that library fine, and as soon as I can get the money, I'll put it back. Maybe I'll be able to collect it today at school."

"I know about the pictures on disk, Maxey." I'd known three whole days now, but I hadn't said anything to her until I'd found the disk and had it safely hidden. Maxey was a pure amateur when it came to hiding things. I found it in her underwear drawer.

I took it, put the disk in plastic wrap and three Ziploc bags, and stuck it in the toilet tank. I checked it yesterday. Still dry as a bone.

Rolling onto her back, she tossed a black jelly bean high into the air and caught it with her mouth. Like a lizard catching flies.

"What pictures?" she asked.

"The ones Marcus gave you on disk," I said, propping up on one elbow. "Of Mr. Constantino and you! Look like a couple of regular lovebirds."

She didn't reply but kept popping jelly beans. And missed two in a row.

"You lied to me about why you needed the money," I said. "Twice! First about Principal Obermeyer needing change, then another lie about the library fine!"

She rolled over and sat up. "So tell on me! Go ahead, Ef."

I glared at her. "Oh, I plan to! I'm still working on the list of all the people I'm going to tell. Number one—"

"Effie," she said, coming over and plopping down on my bed, turning on her Kindly Big Sister routine. "Look, I'm sorry about the money. I thought I'd have it by now. If you want, I can help you go talk to Sister Lucille today. Maybe we could make a deal with her. Tell her to keep quiet about the treasury until we pay it back. If she agrees to that, we won't tell Principal Obermeyer we saw her holding hands with Father McCabe."

"We never saw her holding hands with Father McCabe!"

"Oh, I know. But this is an emergency. We have to keep this from getting to Mom!"

I put my head into my hands. "I should just tell her everything."

Maxey hung her head upside down over the side of my bed and brushed her hair out.

"We-e-ll, you could do that. Then we both get in trouble, and nothing gets solved. I've just about got her fifty percent convinced not to send us to the convent for babysitting. I've got two full days of perfect behavior on my success chart. She said if I got a whole week of stars, she'd reconsider. Don't blow it for us!"

"You'll never make it a whole week," I said.

"Effie, just think about this a second," she said, whipping back upright, her cheeks bright red. "What do you suppose Mom is going to think if you tell her you've lost the whole treasury?"

"I didn't lose it! You stole it, and I know what she's going to think!" I said, almost yelling, my voice strangled. "It's what everyone is going to think if this gets out. That we're just like Dad! Just a couple of rotten crooks—chips off the old block!"

Maxey grabbed the front of my pajamas. "Don't say that! Dad is not a rotten crook! He's a *white-collar criminal*—it's not the same!"

I'd heard my sister say that a million times and it still amazed me the way she could make it sound. Like something very fancy.

For the longest time when I was little, I thought my dad didn't live with us because he was a priest. I got that white-collar part mixed up with the one like Father McCabe wore. In my house we learned about the church before we learned about the rest of the world. And since "criminal" sounds like "cardinal"—well, I was sure Dad had some very important job in the church. Then when I heard Maxey tell some teenage boys down the street that our dad was in the Big House, I thought she meant the Vatican.

"And it wasn't his fault." Maxey sneered at me. "You

don't know anything." She let go of my pajamas and pushed me back. "Dad explained everything to me before he left," she said in the possessive voice she always used when talking about Dad. "It was all Mr. Hocker's fault. Dad didn't know where the money was going."

She pulled her hair up high over her head in a ponytail and yanked a rubber band over it. And wrapped it over and over and over again until her ponytail was so tight I was half expecting her head to explode.

She gave it a final hard crank with two hands. "And if breaking our mother's heart is not enough for you to keep your mouth shut, then you might want to think about what Aurora Triboni will think about all this as well. The Tribonis are almost fanatics about the Scout program. Did you know that Chip, Flint, Buck, and Beau are *all* Wolf Scouts? You know," she said, tapping one finger against her temple, "it might not be a bad idea for me to give Mrs. Triboni a courtesy call about this. I doubt very much she'd want Aurora associating with a Scout treasurer who is responsible for losing close to a hundred dollars."

"You call Mrs. Triboni, Maxey, and I swear you'll live to regret it!" I said, trying to keep my voice mean and not hysterical.

Maxey stuffed her feet into her giant bunny slippers and headed for the bathroom. She paused at the doorway and turned. Four shiny bunny eyeballs stared at me. "Don't you see, Effie? It's better all the way around if we just find a way to fix this. It really is the only choice." She slammed the door behind her as if that settled it.

I threw off my covers like they were to blame and sat on

the edge of my mattress, staring at the computer. My feet dangled off the side of the bed, heavy as bricks. My nose started to tingle and burn like it does right before I'm going to cry. I tried to rub it away. Maxey thought I only had one choice left. She was wrong. I had too many choices. That was the problem.

Some choices made the mess better but made me feel worse. I couldn't find a choice that made the mess better and me feel better. Except the one where I turned us in to Mom, and that would make her feel really bad. I just couldn't pick that one.

I remembered what Mom said about her choice about Dad last night: "It was the last right choice left."

Last right choice left. Last right choice left. It started to hum inside of me. *Last right choice left last right choice left last right choice left last right choice left last right choice left—*

I got up, headed straight for it, my heart beating up against the back of my throat. It was time to take Grandpa to school.

Chapter 16

Two hours later, I sat on the school bus, wearing Mom's raincoat. Mine was lost, and Mom wouldn't let me go out without one. She'd rolled up the sleeves and wrapped the belt around me twice. I looked like a walking tent.

I didn't care how I looked. I was just hoping to survive the day, then get my life back on track. Once I got the money and put it back in the treasury, my life as a crook's helper was over. After four o'clock today, I was planning on becoming a regular saint.

The bus lurched from side to side in the rain and wind, a perfect background to my mood. Today of all days, I had to sit next to Maxey. Philomena Finch was off at the orthodontist, so no one was there to save Maxey a good seat. She held herself scooched close to the window, which was fine with me.

She jabbed me in the side with her pointy elbow. "Hey, Effie," she whispered. "Maybe I could ask Mr. Constantino to loan me twenty bucks." Her eyes grew dreamy. "I could tell him I'd worn out my only pair of ballet shoes from practicing so much and Mom couldn't afford to buy me another pair. How's that sound?"

"If I hear one more word about Mr. Constantino, I am going to upchuck all over this seat," I said. "How's that sound?"

"Well, you're just being a grump." She reached over her seat and opened her backpack. "Dang it!" she swore. "I forgot my lunch." She looked over at my backpack. "What'd you bring today? I'm hungry already." She dragged it over her way.

"Maxey, give it back! It's mine," I said, yanking it from her.

"It's not yours," she said. "It's Mom's food." She pulled it onto her lap.

I tried to wrench it back, but she had a death grip on it.

"Relax, Effie! I just want to get an apple or something to nibble on." With one arm still locked around it, she yanked the zipper open.

"Give-it-here-now!" I said, my teeth clenched. I put both arms around it and pulled with all my strength. The bus took a quick corner, dumping Maxey and me into the aisle. Everything in my backpack spilled out and began rolling away.

"No!" I cried, scrambling after my lunch sack, school-books, comic books, and enough pens and pencils to start my own school.

The bus driver caught the commotion through the rearview mirror. "You girls sit down back there, or I'll have to write you up."

Maxey brushed herself off, her cheeks bright. "I'm telling Mom as soon as we get home that you nearly caused an accident on the bus!" she whispered.

"Oh, no! I can't find my thermos." I dove back under the seat in front of us.

She grabbed the back of my raincoat and pulled me off the floor. "Get up, will you? Everyone's staring at you."

I dug through the bottom of my backpack. "My thermos is gone!"

"So? Big deal! I can't believe you still carry a thermos. Only babies carry thermoses."

I slid down out of my seat and peered down the underside of the row. I didn't see it anywhere. I wriggled over to the next row on my belly and looked down its length. Nothing but tennis shoes and backpacks.

No Star Fleet thermos anywhere.

I snaked my way down the middle aisle of the bus, using my elbows to pull me along. Kinda hoping no one would notice, but not banking on it. It didn't matter. I had to get it back!

"Effie! Get up on this seat right now!" Maxey growled.

I traveled on, my shoulders starting to throb.

HG dropped out of her seat onto all fours next to me. "You okay, Effie? What happened?"

"My thermos rolled out," I said. Our eyes met for a second and I could see her read the panic in mine. "I've got to find it!" I said.

Her eyes darted to the rear of the bus. "Back there," she said.

"EFFELIIIINE!" Maxey barked in the big-sister voice

that was almost impossible to ignore. I looked up at her. She raised my thermos like a trophy. Her smile was dark and sinister.

I ran scrunched over back to our seat, hoping the bus driver wouldn't yell at me again.

Maxey stood and held it over her head. "Want your thermos back, huh?"

I jumped and tried to grab it out of her hand. No luck. She had almost six inches on me. This was Maxey's favorite game, one she had perfected after years of practice.

"You two in the back sit down right *now*. DO YOU HEAR ME?" The bus driver was on his last drop of patience with us.

All eyes turned. Maxey flung her hair over one shoulder and gave them all a queenlike smile. "Just chill out, Effie," she said. "You can have your dumb little thermos back. I just want a drink first." She popped the top off and started to unscrew the cap.

"Don't, Maxey! It's full of—*worms!*" I said in a rush.

She paused and glared at me. But stopped unscrewing the top. She shook the thermos cautiously.

"Packed in dirt to keep them fresh," I said, nearly breathless. "I bought them for my Discovery Project."

Maxey clamped the cup back on top and tossed it over onto my lap.

"You and your little worm friends are in big trouble with me, Effie." She turned toward the window, leaving me to stare at her bony shoulder.

I zipped up my backpack and muttered, "Get in line."

• • •

The inside of our combination auditorium/gym was hot and damp. The windows were all fogged up from too many kids with hot cereal breath. Best friends sat locked in sets of two, like they were inside Noah's Ark. I glanced up at the clock in the back and wiped the rain and sweat off my forehead. Ten more minutes until assembly started.

I went back into the lobby, looking around for Marcus. He'd said to meet him outside assembly, but it was pouring. I leaned up against the window and looked out.

"Hey, Ef! Over here!" Marcus's head popped out of the boys' bathroom.

I looked around to make sure no one was watching and hurried over.

"Quick!" he said. "Come in! We're having it in here!"

"I can't go in the boys' bathroom!" I gasped.

"Ah, don't be such a girl. It's just for a coupla minutes. No one's going to know." He took a quick look around and dragged me in by the arm.

The worst smells in the entire universe all lived in this bathroom. I put my hands over my nose and mouth and gagged. "Omigod! What is that?"

Marcus grinned. "You'll see! So did you bring it?" he asked, rubbing his hands together like Rumpelstiltskin junior.

"Yes," I said, my eyes watering from the stench. "Did you bring my money?"

He pulled a cash wad from his front pocket.

I reached for it, but he whisked it away.

"After the show," he said. He turned and took a quick head count. ". . . eleven, twelve, thirteen, and Ef makes fourteen, but she doesn't count because she's in the show. Okay, did I get everyone's two bucks?"

He plucked the last of the admissions money from the small crowd.

"Hey, Brian," he called to a nervous-looking third grader with one enormous front tooth. "Guard the door, man. Don't let anyone else in!"

Marcus took a small bow and began. "*Ladies* and *Gentlemen,* introducing the first and finest show of its kind at good ol' St. Dom's—Marc's Amazing Marvels and Grossouts!"

"Hurry up, Marc!" Brian whispered. "Somebody is trying to get in." He flattened himself against the door, trying to keep it closed.

"All right, here we go!" Marcus nudged a tiny kid next to him. "Show them what you've got, Nicky!"

The kid reached deep into his pocket and pulled out a small ratty-looking box. He eased the lid off while everyone crowded around.

"Let me see, kid!"

"Hey, move over, you're hogging the view."

"It'th my dog'th infected tooth!" Nicky lisped proudly through his own missing teeth.

I tried not to look, but my eyes had a mind of their own. The tooth was enormous and looked like some kind of dinosaur fossil. Except the tooth was yellow with big red and green scabs on it. I turned my head quick as I could and tried to erase it from my mind. I tried to shut off all air going into my nose. I didn't know how much longer I could take it, standing in what smelled like hell's nightmare.

Someone banged loudly from the outside of the bathroom door. "Let us in!"

Brian's face was turning purple and he grunted, straining to keep the door shut. "Marc, help! They're trying to get in."

Marc marched over to the door and yanked it open. He glared down at a group of startled first graders in giant winter parkas. "You want in? It's two bucks apiece!" He put his palm up under their faces. "Pay up or scram!"

They scattered like mice.

He shut the door and planted himself in front of it. "Okay, I don't think they'll be back!" He licked his lips and smiled. "Now, next in the line of truly awesome grossouts—"

"Next is me!" I interrupted. "I want out of here!" I put my palm under his face. "Pay up now!"

He pulled a couple of scrunched-up twenties from his pocket and handed them to me. "Half now and half at the second show."

"Second show!" I said, shocked.

"Sure, right after school. At the Boys' Club. We'll make a killing there!"

"Forget it, Marc!" I spit, furious. "We had a deal. You never said anything about a second show."

"Sorry, Ef," he said, looking not one bit sorry. "I'm barely going to break even on this one. Gotta do it!"

The boys closed in. "Come on, Ef, show us what you got."

"Yeah, Marc said yours is the coolest! That's why I came," said Kevin.

I drew a thin breath. What air I could get was thick with what smelled like every dirty sock ever worn by a junior high boy, icky boys' bathroom smells, and pepperoni pizza breath—and in the last minute, someone had let go of a deadly, silent fart.

Marcus grabbed my backpack. "It's in here, I bet. Let's see it."

"Back off, Marcus!" I growled through gritted teeth. I suddenly understood completely why nice dogs bite. I could have taken a big mean chunk out of Marcus right then and there. Then I'd like to go find Maxey and take a big bite of her, too. Right on her prissy little butt. I was sick to death of being pushed, tricked, and teased.

"Everybody back off," I barked. "I'm not showing you guys anything unless you give me some room!"

Each kid backed up half an inch. I ripped the zipper open on my pack and reached for my thermos. A deep shiver went down my spine. I'd been trying to convince myself for the last two hours that Grandpa would want me to do this. That it really was my last right choice left. But I hoped he wasn't watching me from heaven.

Even if this was the right choice, I still felt like scum. Lower than scum.

"You guys have to promise right now you won't tell any-body about this," I whispered through clenched teeth. "Once you look in this thermos—if you *ever* speak of it, your tongue will catch on fire! Then," I added in my most sinister voice, "it's gonna dissolve into burnt jam and slide down the back of your throat. You will never, ever speak again."

They nodded with big eyes.

I unscrewed the lid slowly. A toilet flushed, roaring like Niagara Falls behind the stall door. My breath caught in my throat and I dropped the cap. It clattered to the floor as I clamped my hand over the top of the thermos.

All heads turned to glare at a big, freckly kid, who came out buckling his belt.

"Spencer!" they hissed. "There's a girl in here!"

"Wha-at?" he said. "I went behind the door."

"Okay, okay, everyone! Group chill, please," Marcus urged, his voice low. "Effie, let's go! We don't have much time left."

"Someone get me the top first," I said. "It rolled over there under the sink." Nicky handed it to me and I dropped it into my raincoat pocket.

I tried to step back to get some breathing room, but the group clustered closer around me. I felt like I was in the middle of a giant live artichoke and the leaves were squeezing me, cutting off my air.

"Well, what is it? What ya got in there?" Benjamin asked.

I held my hand over the top. I was standing in a nightmare, only I was awake. And I was about ready to be very, very sick. I licked the sweat off my lip. The ground under me felt like it was tilting.

"Ith it alive? Ith it goin' to get out?" Nicky asked, anxious.

"Marcus, wait! I don't think I can—" I started, trying to focus on his face.

"It's her DEAD grandpa!" Marcus hooted. "She's got her grandfather's ashes in there. Show 'em, Ef!"

Thirteen mouths fell open.

I told my hand to move off the top. And squeezed my eyes closed.

Chapter 17

"Hey, that's no fair! We can't see him!" Kevin complained.

"You can too!" I said, indignant, looking down at the eensy viewing space I'd opened between two fingers.

"Effie!" Marcus said. "You gotta take your hand away. These guys paid good money to see it. Now come on!"

The bathroom door heaved and banged behind Marcus. "THIS IS PRINCIPAL OBERMEYER. OPEN THIS DOOR RIGHT NOW."

I looked at the door, horrified.

Marcus yanked the door open a crack to peek and then threw it open wide.

The boys rushed out around him, dodging Principal Obermeyer like little fullbacks.

"Marcus Crenshaw, freeze!" Principal Obermeyer boomed. She collared him as he tried to slide past.

I whipped past her, head down, aiming for the front door of the gym. The storm threw itself at me as I ran outside. It had been a bad storm twenty minutes ago. Now it was a *terrible* storm. The kind nobody should be out in.

The rain slapped me in the face. I could hardly see. I took a big breath and sucked up a bunch of water. I coughed and tried to get to the thermos cap, but Mom's raincoat pockets were somewhere around my knees. I couldn't reach the bottom. I covered the top of the thermos with my hand to keep the ashes dry. The wind pushed and then pulled at me.

Overhead, the sky lit up with a blast of lightning, and then seconds later cracked with thunder.

"MISS MA-LO-NEY!"

I wiped the wet hair out of my eyes and looked back at the gym. Principal Obermeyer stood in the doorway waving me in. I hugged Grandpa close to me.

"Come inside *now!*" she yelled.

I had to get away from her. She looked mad. She'd probably throw me against the wall and frisk me. The bus shelter was just up a way by the flagpole. Three flights of steps and a walkway. I had to get out of the rain for just one second so I could put Grandpa away. And hide him somewhere safe. I couldn't let Principal Obermeyer see what I had.

"Effeliiiiine! Get back in here right now!" a familiar voice screeched.

My head whipped around. Maxey was standing next to Principal Obermeyer, who was fumbling with an umbrella. Oh, no! Principal was coming after me!

My raincoat flapped around me, useless. I looked like a giant duck trying to fly. I tried to close it, but the wind kept ripping it open. Rain fell on me like wet concrete.

I made a run for the bus shelter—up the steps, holding tight to the metal rail for balance. Lightning lit the way, bolt after bolt.

Then the hail came and pounded me. Like somebody was dumping buckets of little white gumballs on me. And then golfballs. I ran faster into the giant wind machine.

"Efffffie!" someone yelled.

"Let go . . . don't touch . . . stop . . . come back!"

Two more flights and I'm there! My feet slid out from under me for a second, but I managed to hook my arm over the rail. I swung there a second like a crazy-looking Christmas tree ornament. I scrambled to my feet and looked back at the gym. Principal Obermeyer was after me, and fast. She had her shoes in her hand and was running in her bare feet. A lot of kids were standing outside the gym doors next to Maxey. They were all screaming. A teacher was holding Maxey, who was trying to break away.

"Lightning . . . don't . . . hold—" Principal Obermeyer yelled.

I tucked my chin over the thermos top to keep it dry. And tightened my death grip on the railing. I took the last two flights two steps at a time.

"Miss Maloney! Take your hands off—"

Off Grandpa? Never.

I clawed my way through the storm, trying to catch a breath. The bus shelter was just feet away, right next to our St. Dominic's flagpole. The place that Maxey told me to go to if I ever got scared or lost. Well, I wasn't lost, but I was *plenty* scared now. Our crazy strict army soldier principal was chasing and screaming at me. This was worse than any bad dream I'd ever had about her.

"Effie, NO!" Maxey's scream cut through the air.

I spun around for one last look behind me. Principal Obermeyer was just a few yards away. Maxey had broken away and was hot on us both.

My foot came down on an icy ball of hail and I slid hard, nearly doing the splits. I held Grandpa over my head so I wouldn't drop him—and with the other hand I grabbed for the flagpole. I dragged myself back up, holding on tight to the pole.

"LET GO OF IT!" Principal screamed at me.

The sky buzzed with white, snaky fire and the world shook with thunder in the very same instant—just the way it happened to Grandpa when he was a boy! I looked up, my face plastered to the side of the wet flagpole. I saw the bolt coming. Saw its long fingers reaching for the pole. The hairs on my neck went stiff like porcupine quills.

Principal Obermeyer came at me like a tank, knocking me down flat on the ground. Then drove her big self up over my backside. Maxey landed on top of her, screaming at us both. My thermos hit the ground with a clunk.

The rain running down the flagpole sizzled like grease on Mom's pancake grill. The pole hummed as a brilliant white bolt stabbed at it. Principal Obermeyer spun us into a triple rollover, whirling us to safety. She spread herself over the two of us.

The thunder was louder than anything I'd ever heard. Principal Obermeyer sheltered our ears as best she could with her arms and her two hands. I could feel Maxey panting against my neck. We lay under Principal for a brief eternity while the storm pounded, crackled, and boomed around us.

And then there was quiet for one blessed moment.

Principal's weight shifted, and I felt her lift her head to look up. I followed her gaze up the flagpole. I sucked in what breath I had. There was a large black burn hole through the flag—right through poor St. Dominic.

"Oh, dear God!" Principal Obermeyer looked back down at me. She moved off us quickly, then knelt over me. I struggled to get up, but she pushed me back down, smoothing the wet hair out of my eyes.

"*Lie still! Don't move yet!*" she shouted. She peered into my eyes, then grabbed my wrist to feel my pulse.

"It didn't get me," I said, feeling shocked all the same. And I was trying to hold on to something important that had been jolted right out of my mind.

"Are you all right? Can you hear me?" Principal asked, her eyes worried.

Maxey came into my view, peering down at me. "Effie, where the *hell* were you going?" she swore right in front of—

"My THERMOS!" I screamed in her face, fighting to get up.

I rolled over and out of their grasp and struggled to my feet. I could see it. It had fallen off the curb, into the street. I staggered over, my head swimmy, and dropped down in front of it. I mopped the rain out of my eyes so I could see inside.

It was empty. Nothing but a few dark grains left in its mouth. And an ashy river that was my grandpa was flowing down the street.

Principal Obermeyer came up behind me, tried to pull me out of the street. "Leave it, Effeline, let's get—"

I wriggled away from her, tried to scoop up the wet trail of ashes with my hands, but the rain carried it faster than I could grab it. My hands were full of nothing. He was gone, and there was nothing left of him for me to keep.

An animal-like howl started somewhere in a deep-down part of me. And it ripped me all the way up.

Maxey squatted down next to me. "Effie! Let the worms go. It's okay, I'll explain to Mr. Giles about your project."

"NO-OOOOO-OOOO!" I shouted. "It's not worms, Maxey! It's *Grandpa!*"

She stared at me, her eyes huge, like I'd just stepped right off the deep end.

Principal Obermeyer reached over me—this time with soft, strong hands. She lifted me toward her like a baby. Like I didn't weigh anything at all. She turned my head toward her chest, shielding me from the rain.

She began to run.

The world went dark, and I fell into it.

Chapter 18

Soft music was playing, the lights were dim, and I was cocooned in an enormous quilt when I finally woke up at 10:32 a.m. According to the clock hanging above Principal Obermeyer's desk.

I closed my eyes a moment to try and make sense of it all. When I opened them again at 10:33 a.m., Principal Obermeyer was perched on a chair next to the couch where I was lying. I couldn't help noticing right away that her panty hose were ripped and her knees were all scraped up. She turned down the small electric heater next to me.

"You're fine," she whispered. "Safe and fine. Not a single lightning bolt hole on you. Though you came very, very close, young lady," she added, putting her hand on her chest and taking a deep breath.

I licked my lips and tried to wake up. "Wha—?"

"Take it easy, Miss Maloney. You've had a pretty big morning." She smoothed the covers over me, even though they were already perfect.

"I tried to call your mother," she said, "but some of our phone lines are down. We'll try again in a little bit." She reached for my wrist and put her index and middle fingers on my pulse, then checked her watch.

"Are you a nurse?" I asked, my voice scratchy.

"A medic," she said. "Back when I was in the army."

"I'm really sorry about your panty hose and everything."

"Don't even worry about it. I hate this color anyway. I was just looking for an excuse to throw them away."

I bit my lip and tried to smile, studying her face. I'd never really seen her up close before. She wasn't pretty, but she had these gray-bluey eyes that were nice. Like my best broken-in jeans.

"How come I'm—in here?" I asked.

"The power went out in the infirmary. Seemed best to bring you here since we couldn't get your mom yet."

I guess that made sense. But I bet I was the first kid ever to lie on Principal Obermeyer's couch. I saw my clothes hanging over a chair. My shoes were under the chair.

And next to them, my thermos.

"Did I pass out or something?" I asked, confused.

She smiled and shook her head. "No, you just took a little nap of sorts. It's the body's way of protecting a person when she's had a big shock. Not an electric shock," she corrected herself quickly. "But sometimes a person just needs to go inside herself for a while."

Something hot burned behind my eyes.

Principal Obermeyer looked over her shoulder, then back at me. "Want to tell me about your thermos?"

My eyes stung and I closed them hard. I shook my head. I just wanted to go back to sleep.

"Might make you feel better to talk about it," she continued.

When I didn't answer, she went on. "You know, your big sister has been very worried about you."

I wiped my eyes, which were starting to leak. Maxey worried about *me* seemed unbelievable.

"She begged me to stay with you, but she was making such a ruckus I was afraid she'd disturb you."

I opened my eyes for a moment. "What was she upset about?"

Principal Obermeyer handed me a tissue. "Well, among other things, she blamed herself that she'd never told you to stay away from metal during an electrical storm. She felt particularly responsible that you'd run to the flagpole for safety."

I swallowed hard.

She leaned forward in her chair. It creaked. "She told me all about the money, Effeline."

My mouth opened, but I couldn't find a voice to go with it.

"In fact," she said with a small smile, "I couldn't get Maxine to stop confessing all the things she'd done to you. I finally called Father McCabe to come over and listen to her for a while. She had a lot to unload."

Principal Obermeyer checked her watch again, then

tucked my hand back under the covers. "I had a big sister growing up. I think I have a pretty good idea what you've been going through here."

She pulled a small square of paper from her pocket. "She left you a note and made me promise to give it to you as soon as you woke up. Feel like reading it?"

"Oh . . . kay, I guess." Maxey had folded it several times plus some, so it took a while to get to it. In my whole life, I'd never gotten a letter, or even a note, from my sister. I bent my knees up under the quilt and spread it out so I could see it better.

Dear Effie,

I'm very sorry you almost got hit by lightning. Don't EVER go to the flagpole in a storm. I saw you running for it and I knew you must have needed me and I couldn't get there in time. Dad would kill me if anything happened to you. I promised him when he left that I'd always look out for you.

I miss Grandpa, too, Ef—guess that's why I still put candy under our pillows. I like to pretend he's still around. But don't tell Mom about the candy, okay?

I hope you're not having a nervous breakdown or anything.

Your big sister,
Maxine Colleen Maloney

The phone jingled softly on Principal Obermeyer's desk. She reached over to grab it. "Excuse me a moment, Effeline. Yes, Helen, who is it?" She paused a moment, nodding. "Fine. I'll tell her. Oh, okay, hold on." She covered the mouthpiece a moment. "Would you like some hot chocolate?"

I nodded dumbly, still in shock about Maxey spilling the beans on herself, and her note to me. It was *her* putting the candy under my pillow all these months.

"Thanks, Marge. Bring me one too." She hung up the phone. "My assistant finally got through to your mom. She's coming right over and bringing you and Maxey some dry clothes."

My cheeks flamed, and I peeked under the covers to see what I was wearing. I hoped to heaven I wasn't naked in the principal's office. I'd had a nightmare about that back in second grade after I accidentally forgot to wear underpants to school one day.

I had on a giant soft gray sweatshirt. Had some kind of army design on it, but it was hard to tell looking upside down.

"My gym sweats," she said. "Nurse Nikki changed you out of your wet clothes. Do you remember?"

I bit my lip and tried to pull up Nurse's face from the morning. The trouble with remembering was you couldn't just go after one detail like that. Once you started, it all came back. I think Principal Obermeyer must have known that and asked me that on purpose.

A giant hot tear burned its way down my cheek.

Dribbled onto my neck and pooled up in a skin fold there. "Grandpa's ashes," I choked.

She cupped her chin in her hand. "Go on," she said.

"I brought them to school to show some kids." I sucked in a tight breath and continued with a whisper. "For *money*."

She nodded, quiet. "So I heard."

Chapter 19

Mr. Giles's afternoon class had already started by the time I joined them after lunch. Felt like I'd been away to another planet and back since the morning. When Mom came to school to pick me up, I begged her to let me stay. I didn't want to let Aurora Triboni down on Discovery Project day.

But Mom took Maxey home. It was Father McCabe's idea. Said Maxey had had a "rather exhausting confession" and needed to take a little time out. Mom said she and I would talk later.

All heads whipped toward me when I walked in, and my classmates went wild. In just a few hours, I'd become a celebrity.

"Hey, it's Lightning Rod!"

"Effie, did you really die and come back to life?" Naomi asked.

"Can we see your raincoat? A boy in fifth grade says it has a big burn hole right through it."

"Man, did you guys see when Principal Obermeyer jumped on her and rolled her away? That was the coolest!"

Mr. Giles tried to bring back some order. "Children! Quiet! One at a time, please."

I slinked to my seat and sat down.

"Do you think Principal Obermeyer will let you keep the burnt flag? You know, kind of as a souvenir?" Naomi asked.

Mr. Giles walked to the doorway and turned off all the lights. That was his special signal for "everyone quiet now."

"Now, class, Miss Maloney has already had a very exciting morning. Let's give her a little time, shall we? Perhaps after all our projects are presented, she'll feel up to sharing her experience with us."

I smiled weakly at him, grateful for the break.

"Now! Back to our Discovery Projects, yes?" he asked. "Effeline, you've only missed one. We had an interesting baking project by the Frasier twins. Chocolate-dipped vegetables. We were all just sampling their chocolate-covered Brussels sprouts when you joined us."

HG turned around and gave me a small wave. And offered me some of hers.

I shook my head, smiled back at her. "Hey, thanks for trying to help me on the bus this morning," I whispered.

She grinned back and blushed.

I waited for Aurora Triboni to turn around and say hi. But she sat facing forward, stiff as a mummy. Maybe she was having a case of nerves about our project.

Mr. Giles checked his clipboard, cleared his throat. "The

next Discovery Project will be presented by Kayla Quintana, and—let's see, no, that's not right. Miss Quintana? Who's your partner? I'm a bit confused."

Kayla grabbed a gym bag from under her desk and hurried up to the front. "Aurora Triboni," she announced. "She's my partner."

My stomach dropped like a rock off a ten-story building.

Kayla stood at the front of the classroom and gave Aurora a long stare. Like she was challenging her to deny it.

Mr. Giles scratched his head with his pen. "Now, I'm confused. Aurora, didn't you tell me on Monday that you and Effeline were partners?"

"They were," Kayla said, smug. "But Aurora changed her mind. Right, Aurora?"

Everyone did a major rubberneck and stared back at me and Aurora.

She unfolded her legs and moved stiffly to the blackboard. She stared down at her folder and licked her lips.

HG slammed her Bible shut and muttered something.

"Well, then, girls?" Mr. Giles asked. "Tell us what you've discovered!"

Aurora opened her folder and recited in a mouse-sized voice, "Our discovery is a kid-friendly toilet-seat cover."

Not true! This *ab-so-lute-ly* could not be true! This had to be a very, very bad dream. Maybe I was still asleep on Principal Obermeyer's couch, having a nightmare.

"What'd she say?" asked a kid in back. "A kitty toilet warmer?"

"Aurora," Mr. Giles interrupted. "A little louder, please."

Kayla jumped in with her bounciest pep club voice. "We invented the first-ever kid-friendly toilet-seat cover! Show 'em, Aurora!" Kayla shot me a look that dared me to contradict her.

Aurora reached into Kayla's bag and pulled out our invention. The one that we had made together just days ago. She held it up over her head while Kayla pointed out all the "really fabulous features."

"Hey, that's pretty cool," Naomi said. "I hate when those things won't stay."

"Now we'll pass out the samples," Kayla continued, "and Aurora will give a live scientific demonstration. Well, not completely live," she said, trying to kiss up to Mr. Giles, "but enough so you get the idea."

Kayla's fan club giggled, like she was some kind of comedian.

I just sat there with my mouth open.

Kayla scooted a trash can over to the front of the class and laid Mr. Giles's large atlas on top. "We'll pretend this is a toilet. Is that okay, Mr. Giles?"

He stood in the corner, arms crossed, one hand over his mouth. He nodded.

Aurora went to the head of each row, handing out samples. They'd made a ton of them, enough for everybody. Guess that's why she'd been too busy to call me while I was out sick Monday and Tuesday. She and Kayla had a regular toilet-seat-cover factory going. Probably used up every last one of my mom's mini-pads.

"When you get your sample toilet-seat cover, class,"

Kayla said in her most grown-up voice, "you can try it at your desk."

Like a robot, Aurora leaned over the pretend toilet, pulled the sticky strips off the seat cover, pasted it to the atlas, and sat down. She stared at her big black tennies.

Kayla picked up Aurora's folder and began to read. "The first disposable toilet-seat cover was invented in—"

A blast of laughter from a group of boys drowned out the rest of Kayla's speech.

"Excuse me, I'm trying to read our report!" she said, indignant.

"Boys, if you have comments or questions, kindly raise your hand," Mr. Giles said. "I'm sure we'll all enjoy hearing your thoughts."

One of the Frasier twins raised his hand. "Um, I have a question."

"Ye-es?" Kayla asked.

His pals tittered, and he turned to shush them, grinning. "These stick-on pads. Aren't they, um, you know, special pads for mothers?"

Kayla rolled her eyes and planted a hand on her hip. "They are called mini-pads and they are for girls when they—"

"Whoa, whoa, now!" Mr. Giles broke in. "Kayla, thank you, but let's leave that for next year's health science class." He rubbed his palms together. "Other comments, please. Class, what do you think? Could this sell?"

HG raised her hand.

"Miss Finch, yes? Your thoughts?"

"When they designed this, they did away with the punched-out center part." She held up her sample and poked her hand through it. "See? Nothing's there."

Kayla crossed her arms across her chest, smug. "That's what makes this kid-friendly. We did all the work for you. No more middle to try to tear out!"

"But you need that punched-out part," HG said.

"You do?" several kids asked. They turned to her.

"Sure," she said. "It's that punched-out center hanging down that gets caught in the flush cycle. Once it gets wet, it's heavy enough to pull the seat cover off and down the drain."

She stopped for effect and raised one eyebrow. "It's so you don't have to touch the seat cover after you use it. It's an important hygiene feature."

Kayla narrowed her eyes at Aurora, like she should have known that.

It had certainly never occurred to me.

"And one more thing," HG continued. "You're not allowed to flush these mini-pads glued on the back. They'll plug up your toilet. My cousin Brittany was staying at our house once, and she was having her, you know—"

"Thank you, Miss Finch!" Mr. Giles cut her off. "And," he said, coming back to the front of the classroom, "thank you Kayla and Aurora for your invention! Some design kinks to work out, perhaps, but nonetheless a fascinating idea."

Aurora slunk back to her seat. Kayla pressed her lips into a thin line and zipped up her gym bag.

"Class, next on our list we have Trinity Finch," Mr. Giles said, looking over the top of his glasses. "Trinity, you never told me who your partner was going to be. I made a note here that you said it was going to be a surprise." His voice trailed off and he looked at her expectantly.

HG stood up and announced to the class. "It's Effie. My partner is Effie Maloney."

Which broke right through the coma I'd been in for the past ten minutes.

HG turned back toward me, motioned me with her head to follow. And gave me a look that simply said, "Trust me."

Chapter 20

My head was swimming by the time I got to the front of the classroom. I wished I were home with Mom. Heck, even being home with Maxey sounded good right now. I looked out over the class and caught Aurora's eye. She looked completely shocked that I was HG's partner.

Not half as shocked as I was.

HG pulled out several packs of wintergreen LifeSavers and passed out a pack to each row leader. "Take one Life-Saver, and then pass the roll back. As soon as you get yours, go ahead and start sucking on it, okay?"

Kids sat up in their seats.

HG handed me one. "Suck," she said.

I popped it into my mouth and felt the familiar burning on my tongue and gums.

She put her hands in her pockets and cleared her throat. "Effie and I have been conducting a scientific experiment on body temperature for months." She gave me a soft elbow to my side. "Tell them, Effie, about the important experiments you have been conducting at home."

I blew out a tingly gust and locked eyes with her. In that second, we had a silent conversation about whether I was willing to give up my secret. And then I realized stupidly that HG was giving up her secret too. I remembered Maxey's voice from this morning—*Philomena says HG can do it too*. And HG was willing to give it up so I'd have a Discovery Project and not be totally humiliated by Aurora and Kayla.

HG handed me our written report. Across the top, it read:

WINTERGREEN FEVER SAVES LIVES
by Effeline C. Maloney and Trinity M. Finch

A chill tiptoed across the back of my neck. But, at this point, I didn't even question how she'd known that I was going to need a partner and a project. She'd just known. Which maybe wasn't so spooky after all. It was just very, very cool.

I looked up from the cover sheet. "Thanks, Trinity," I said in a quiet voice just meant for us. I faced the class and cleared my throat. "Very few people know this, but sucking on a wintergreen LifeSaver can make your temperature go up."

Several kids in class put their hands on their foreheads to check their temps.

"We actually think now," HG interrupted, "that it's not that your whole body temperature goes up, but just that the temperature in your mouth kinda heats up for a couple of minutes."

"Yes, that's what we think now," I added. HG smiled at me.

She pulled out a thermometer and gave it a good shake. "In just a minute, we'll take Effie's temperature and demonstrate this."

Mr. Giles piped up from the side of the room. "I'm interested in the scientific research at home, Effie. Can you tell us more about that?"

Brother, this was a banner day for confessions at St. Dominic's. I guess one more couldn't hurt.

"I've been able to fake sick a few times using this, um—"

"Scientific method," HG coached.

"Right! I get my mom to take my temperature right after I have had some wintergreens. My temperature would be about 99.5 degrees or a little higher, so she'd keep me home."

"Effectively proving our hypothesis!" HG said, triumphant.

"And I'm sure this was all done for the sake of science?" Mr. Giles asked.

"Absolutely, sir," HG replied. "This information could save lives."

He took off his glasses and crossed his arms. "Save lives?"

HG popped the thermometer into my mouth and picked up her notes.

"When people go to donate blood, they have to have a normal temperature or they won't be allowed to donate. The blood bank people don't want sick people giving blood, right?"

She paused at the board and wrote "Wintergreen Fever" in giant letters. "Well, imagine if the blood bank knew about Wintergreen Fever! If a blood donor comes in with a temperature, instead of just sending them home, they could check them for very fresh breath. And, if the donor does have very fresh breath, then they can ask them if they had any wintergreens before they came in."

HG paced back and forth across the front of the room like one of those lawyer guys on TV. "And if they have had some," she said, "then instead of turning the donor away, the blood bank can just wait a few minutes and retest. The donor's temperature will go down in a few minutes."

She stopped. "And the fewer donors they have to turn away, the better. The more blood they can collect, the more lives will be saved!"

I looked at her, amazed. That was the longest speech I'd ever heard from her.

"*Nicely* done, Miss Finch," Mr. Giles said, clapping his hands. "What an interesting discovery this is!" He rejoined us at the front of the class. "And I trust now that you've proved your theory, Miss Maloney, you won't need to conduct any more 'scientific research' with your poor mother?" he asked.

I nodded, trying to keep the thermometer balanced under my tongue.

The class laughed.

"In addition to sharing the information with the blood bank, girls," he said, "I would suggest you write up a Wintergreen Fever Alert for the parents of this class."

The kids moaned, "Aw, Mr. Giles . . ."

HG pulled the thermometer out of my mouth and studied it.

"Ninety-nine point nine!" she said.

My almost-best-friend-who-double-crossed-me, Aurora Triboni, started the clapping.

Then the whole class joined in. Real loud. Well, except for Kayla Quintana. She gave Aurora a look that could scare the warts off a witch.

Aurora kept clapping anyway. Then some kids started chanting, *"Rockdale! Rockdale!"* like they thought we should win the trip to the museum.

Kayla leaned over and spit her LifeSaver onto the floor.

HG, I mean, *Trinity,* grabbed my hand. We each took a deep winterfresh breath and bowed.

Chapter 21

On Friday morning of the longest week of my life—the one where I was almost nailed by a lightning bolt and lost my grandpa for good—I found myself again in Principal Obermeyer's office, but this time I was sitting, not lying, and I definitely had my panties on.

And I wasn't alone. In fact, it was near standing room only.

There was me, Maxey, and Mom; then Philomena and Mr. Finch, because Mrs. Finch couldn't leave her job on two-for-one makeover day at Dillard's; then there was the Booger Boy himself, Marcus Crenshaw, and his parents, who looked like pretty regular people except for the fact that Mrs. Crenshaw had a small dog in her purse; and then there was Sister Lucille, who, of course, didn't bring her parents or anything.

Sitting right smack in the middle of Principal's desk was the treasury cash box. I wondered if Principal Obermeyer had enough toothbrushes for all of us, because I had a feeling when this was all over, we were all going to be in big trouble and sentenced to Clean the Latrine duty.

Principal Obermeyer cleared her throat and everyone settled down. She had her palms together under her chin like she was praying, but I knew she wasn't. I was betting that it was her lecture pose.

"Coach Maloney, Mr. Finch, Mr. and Mrs. Crenshaw, Sister Lucille—I truly appreciate your coming today. I know that you all need to get back to your work, so let's get right down to this."

Everyone squirmed in their seats a bit.

"As some of you know by now, there's been a reported theft from the Scout treasury box."

Sister Lucille gasped, "Oh, no, but—"

Principal Obermeyer silenced her with a look and then continued. "Effeline tells me that exactly eighty-seven dollars was taken from the box sometime before the last Scout meeting on Friday. Eighty-seven dollars is a very large amount of money."

"It would feed an entire Guatemalan family for two months." Sister Lucille butted in. "At least," she said, getting kind of red in the face, "that's what Father McCabe says."

"Thank you, Sister," Principal said. "Effeline, it was eighty-seven dollars, correct?" she asked.

I nodded and licked my lips.

"And, the only two people with keys to the treasury are you and Sister Lucille."

Sister Lucille and I looked at each other and nodded.

"However," Principal continued, and then looked dead-on at Maxey, "Maxey and Effeline have both told me that on Friday at lunchtime, under some duress, Effeline gave the treasury keys to Maxey. Is that correct?"

"Oh, Effie—" Sister Lucille started.

Principal gave Sister Lucille a "quiet down *now*" look. Sister pressed her lips together hard.

Maxey lowered her eyes. "Yes, ma'am. I lied to Effie about needing to make some change for you and took the keys from her so I could borrow some money from the treasury. It was a very, very bad thing to do," she added hurriedly, looking at Mom.

Mom looked down at her. "Maxey, we talked about this already. It isn't called borrowing, is it?"

Maxey's face and even the tips of her ears turned very red. She sighed. "I mean I stole the money," she said. "You can't 'borrow' without someone's permission. It was stealing."

Mom reached over and took Maxey's hand. Mom's face was bright red too. I knew this was harder on her than on anybody else in the room.

"Maxey," Principal Obermeyer said, "I want you to look right at your sister, the elected treasurer, the person chosen by St. Dominic's to safeguard this money, and tell her exactly how much you stole."

Maxey turned in her seat and looked at me. "It's like I always told you, Effie. I stole twenty dollars. I don't know what happened to the rest."

"Principal Obermeyer." Sister Lucille broke in. "If I may speak—"

"Sister, I'll get to you shortly," she said.

"Maxey," Principal went on, "was anyone with you when you stole this money?"

Maxey got real quiet. She started swinging her leg. She chewed her nail and then checked the hem of her uniform.

"Maxey?" Mom asked. "We want the whole truth from you."

She looked up at Principal. "Can I take the Fifth Amendment?"

"Max-*ine!*" Mom said, on the fast track to getting pretty mad.

"Okay! Okay!" Phil broke in. "Geez, next you'll be pulling her fingernails out. I was there. I saw her take the money. And I guess I got some stuff from this, too. But, I only saw her take twenty. Swear to—"

"Stop it right there, Philomena," Mr. Finch said. "Let's not pull our poor Father in heaven into this sorry mess!" He took his checkbook from his pocket. "Looky here, Mrs. Oberhagen—"

"Principal Obermeyer," she corrected, her voice very principal-ish.

"Sorry, ma'am. Let's just have all the parents here write a check for a third of the loss—let's see, eighty-seven divided by three would be, say—"

"Twenty-nine dollars!" Sister Lucille chimed, unable to resist a math problem.

"Mr. Finch, please put your checkbook away," Principal said. "This is not a money problem. This is an honesty and responsibility problem that can't be solved by you all writing checks for your children."

She tapped her pen on her tablet. "Now, I need to know who else had access to the treasury box keys. Maxey, could anyone else have seen you open the box or know where your keys were that afternoon?"

"Well," she said, darting a quick look at Booger Boy, "Marcus saw me and Phil go into the closet and was hanging around. And the keys were on the outside of my backpack. He could have gotten in there. But, really, I suppose anyone could have."

"Marcus? Is there something you'd like to tell us?" Principal asked.

"Yeah, well, I feel really bad about Effie losing her grandpa and all and she probably never would have brought the ashes to school if she didn't need the money so bad." He reached into his jeans and pulled out some bills. He stood up and came over to me. "Here, Effie. This is all the money I got in the world. You can put it back in the treasury, and there's some extra, too." He dropped a load of cash into my lap. "Sorry 'bout your grandpa."

He sat back down and looked at Principal. "I didn't take any money out of the treasury. I saw Phil and Maxey in there, and it would have been easy to go in after them. But, I'm not a thief. I like to earn my dough fair and square."

"So where'd you get all that money?" Maxey asked, nodding over at the windfall on my lap.

I was still too stunned to speak. I'd never seen so much cash.

He shrugged.

"Well, he'll never brag on himself, so I guess this is my chance," Mrs. Crenshaw said. "Marcus earns extra money modeling boys' clothes for catalogs."

"Mo-om," he said. "You said you'd never tell!" He slumped in his seat.

"And sometimes . . . ," she said, her voice going all lovey-dovey as she reached into her purse. She pulled out a handful of fur. "Sometimes he models with my widdle Sweet-ums Weet-ums. They have matching tuxes and it's so cute, I could just die!"

Phil clapped her hand over her mouth but you could still hear her snickering.

"Mother!" Mr. Crenshaw said. "Put that flea bucket away, will you?"

Principal Obermeyer took her glasses off and gave them a vigorous cleaning. "Well, then, we're back to square one, I suppose. Sister Lucille, do you have anything to add that might shed some light on this for us? It seems clear to me that none of these children here took the sixty-seven missing dollars."

"Well, are you sure it's missing?" she asked, her voice breathy. "I mean, Effie, when is the last time you actually looked inside the treasury box?"

"Not since the Scout meeting," I said, puzzled.

"Principal Obermeyer? May I?" She stood up and walked over to the desk, pulling her key ring from deep inside her long black pocket. She put the little key in the lock and the lock snapped open; then she pulled the lid up.

"See?" she said, a big smile on her face. "It's all there."

We all leaned forward out of our chairs and looked. Sure enough, the box was loaded with cash—tens, fives, and a ton of crumpled ones. Just like before.

Principal Obermeyer stood up and came around the desk. She perched on the edge and stared hard at Sister Lucille. "Sister? Perhaps, then, you'll be so kind as to explain to these poor children and their parents why you took the money last Friday."

Sister Lucille crossed her arms under the big black bib of her habit, and scraped her lower lip with her teeth.

Chapter 22

Maxey and I stared at my reflection in the mirror. Then we each grabbed a bunny clip and pulled them out of my hair.

"Ow-ow-ouch!" I yelled, then sighed. "Do you think Mom will ever stop trying to make me wear bunny barrettes?" I asked.

"Nope!" Maxey said with a grin, shaking up a big silver can of mousse. "She's got some already picked out for the day you get married. The bunnies are wearing little wedding gowns."

"Very funny!"

Maxey aimed the nozzle at my head, then squirted gobs of white foam round and round my hair, higher and higher.

"Maxey, stop—enough!" I yelled. My head looked like one of the Swiss Alps.

"Oh, just hush, Effie," she said, rubbing her palms together. "Trust me—I know what I'm doing."

I closed my eyes and let her have at it. Mom bought us

an extra-large can of mousse so Maxey wouldn't put toothpaste in my hair anymore. I ought to at least give her a chance.

My sister had been practicing a lot lately at Casa Serena Rescue Mission, where she and I were serving three months' time. After Mom worked her way through all the stories, lies, thefts, safe burglaries, and confessions, she figured it would take about a hundred hours of dishwashing to get our souls back in shape. We go every Saturday, and if we get done doing all the dishes in time, Maxey likes to offer shampoo and hairstyling to the homeless people there. So she's been getting a lot of experience taming wild hair like mine.

Sister Lucille works at the rescue mission with us on Saturdays too. Principal Obermeyer insisted, on account of all the trouble Sister Lucille caused by taking sixty-seven dollars out of the treasury. Even if she only meant to borrow it for a few hours until she got her paycheck at three o'clock.

Turns out that while Maxey was out that day buying a disk from Fashion Boy (who used to be Booger Boy) with money from the treasury, Sister Lucille was out buying Father McCabe a new slide projector with treasury money so he could raise lots of money for the missions in Guatemala.

Mom said even Dad figured he was "borrowing" the money from his clients when he and Mr. Hocker moved money around in the accounts to make more money. But he ended up going to prison. Mom said that Sister Lucille and Maxey just ended up at the rescue mission and they should be grateful.

I didn't exactly come out smelling like a rose either, but Principal let me keep my key to the treasury, with my promise not to ever give it to anyone else. The other key she and I tucked way behind the statue of the Blessed Mother in church for safekeeping. That was my idea and she thought it was a good one.

Even though I got in trouble with Mom for Wintergreen Fever, for breaking into her safe, and for riding my bike into Tiger Town to the pawnshop, I didn't get in trouble for keeping Grandpa's ashes. She cried when I told her about hiding him all those months in my thermos, and wrapped me in an enormous hug, which I hadn't had from her in a long time. She wasn't even mad about me spilling them in the storm. I'd never even seen my mom cry before. But it was the good kind of crying where you feel all cleaned out afterward. That night she took me and Maxey to Grandpa's favorite swanky restaurant and we got to order whatever we wanted. And Mom ordered deep-fried armadillo toenails like he always did to make us laugh.

Maxey turned on the hairdryer to turbo speed and blew a hot blast right in my ear. "Sorry!" she shouted when I jumped.

She shut down the dryer and came around to the front of me. She was already dressed for the ceremony, and I could see she'd put a little something extra in her top. She wasn't lopsided, but she was extremely poofy.

No way she'd ever make it past Mom.

"Here's another thing you better remember, Ef. NEVER use a hairdryer if you are in the bathtub—or standing in a bucket of water."

I rolled my eyes at her. For weeks, she'd been following me around the house reciting safety tips to me. Especially ones about lightning. Like never talk on the phone during a storm. And don't do the dishes in front of an open window when there's lightning. And absolutely no golfing, fishing, or sitting in a metal canoe during a storm.

"Okay, Maxey, but could you just please finish my hair? It's almost time and I still look like a giant marshmallow."

She turned the dryer back on and got to work, giving me some blessed moments of quiet.

It had been four weeks since the lightning hit St. Dominic's, and Maxey had barely let me out of her sight. I heard Mom talking to Principal Obermeyer on the phone about it. She said Maxey had probably wished me dead so many times in her life, that seeing me nearly get skewered by lightning scared her witless. Maxey's new goal in life is to keep me alive.

I wondered if I'd be able to survive it.

But at least it was enough to convince Mom she could try leaving us home alone together "on a trial basis" while she works some extra basketball games for money. Maxey and I sit in the living room still as statues while she is gone so we don't get in trouble with each other and have to get sent to the convent for babysitting.

Maxey shut off the hairdryer and rooted around in the drawer by the sink. "Here they are," she said, pulling out a pair of scissors. "Hold real still, Ef. I'm just going to trim your hair up a bit in back."

I whirled around and glared at her. "No!"

"But I'm just going to take a bit—"

"No for the *second* time, Maxey!"

"I promise you'll love it!"

"This is the *third* no—you know what that means!" I said, baring my teeth.

She dropped the scissors back into the drawer like they were on fire. "Oh, well, fine! I was just trying to help."

Maxey was on a new and improved success chart. It's bigger, and Mom even laminated it. She made me one too. Now, if Maxey doesn't mind me after I tell her no three times, she loses one of her stars, and I get it for my chart. Plus, I get a star for telling Mom, and another one for "setting boundaries."

I racked up a lot of stars the first two weeks, but lately they've been harder to get. Maxey is catching on.

Maxey took one last twirl with the styling brush on my bangs and gave it a good hot blast.

"There!" she said. She fussed around the front of me a moment, then stood back, one eye squinted, like an artist.

I looked around her in the mirror. Truth be told, I looked pretty sensational.

"You know," she said, "I think we should pierce your ears."

"No thanks!" I said, ducking past her. I went into our closet and rummaged around for my good shoes.

Mom shouted up the stairs. "Girls, Trinity and Philomena are here! Let's get going."

That would be Trinity Finch, my new official true-blue-friends-till-we-die best friend. I call her Nit—it's short for Trinity. She likes it.

Nit finally stopped carrying that big Bible around with her. When I asked her how come, she said she'd finally finished reading it. Took her three years. Now she's studying the *Complete History of Vampires*. But she always makes sure she wears a big cross and eats a lot of the garlicky mashed potatoes at the cafeteria.

I actually have two best friends now. One full-fledged, and one on probation—Aurora Triboni. Aurora double-crossed me pretty big. I was ready to write her off forever, but Nit reminded me that her having Kayla Quintana for a best friend had sort of been like having a bossy big sister. Even though Aurora and Kayla had been on the outs, Kayla still knew how to make Aurora jump.

So Nit says we shouldn't be too hard on Aurora. Because we all used to be under someone else's spell. Nit used to be bossed around by her big sister, Phil. That is, until Nit put a vampire curse on her. (Well, she didn't really, but Phil got an enormous oozing zit the night of Winter Hip Hop that Nit predicted. Phil has been behaving very nicely toward Nit since then.)

Maxey came into the closet, where I was putting my shoes on. She sat down next to me, holding a small box. Then she pulled the lid off and showed it to me.

I looked at her, puzzled, poked my finger at it. "What's that—a walnut on a rope?"

"No, Ef! It's *soap* on a rope—it used to be a football, but it's almost used up."

"So?" I asked, trying to cram my foot into my shoe.

"It was Dad's soap on a rope. I saved it for him." Maxey's voice got very small, like something you could frighten away if you weren't very quiet and still.

I turned and looked at her. "O-o-hhh." I looked at it again. "That was really nice of you to save it for him," I said, real soft.

"Yeah, well, I thought for the longest time he'd be coming back." She sighed hard.

I sighed too, and leaned into her a minute like she used to let me do when we were little.

"Mom won't have him back, though," I whispered. " 'Not ever,' she says."

"Oh, I know," she said with a shrug and a big soft breath. "I was just a kid when I saved it. Kinda forgot I had it," she said, putting the lid back on. "I was just showing it to you 'cos it's sort of like you saving Grandpa's ashes. Didn't want you to feel like a total freak about that." She rewrapped the box in an ancient bunny undershirt that had permanent fold lines in it. Then tied an old faded ribbon back around it.

A familiar pointy hip came into our view. "What ya two sitting in the closet for?" Philomena Finch asked.

Maxey shoved the box into the corner and stood up, pulling me, too.

"Just looking for shoes," I said. "Where's Nit?"

"She's downstairs. Your mom is showing her that thing—you know, the memorial whatyamacallit."

"The plaque, Phil?" I asked, patientlike.

"Yeah, *that*," she said.

Phil went over to the mirror on the wall and checked out her backside. "Does this dress look okay, Max? Do I have a panty line? I didn't know what to wear to this— this, well, what is this?"

"It's a dedication ceremony, Phil," Maxey said. "I've told you about eight times."

"Are there going to be any boys there from our school?" she asked.

Maxey stepped in front of Phil's view in the mirror, turned, and looked at her backside. After girls turn twelve, they get very interested in their rear view.

"No, mostly family and a few friends. Well, and Principal Obermeyer."

Phil shuddered. "Why does she have to come? She's so, you know—"

Maxey whirled, then dragged Phil into the bathroom and slammed the door. Then proceeded to tell Phil off in a loud whisper. About how nobody in this house says anything bad about Principal Obermeyer. And could she *please* watch her mouth in front of me?

Maxey still isn't completely convinced I didn't have a nervous breakdown.

I had something all right, but it wasn't that. I think that storm dumped a load of something on me. Don't know whether it's good luck or what Father McCabe calls grace. (Not the praying for dinner kind, but the holy present kind.) It feels like spring inside me and it's still the dead of winter. I guess I'm just seeing things different.

Take Principal Obermeyer, for example. She still walks

very fast, with excellent posture, and scares the first graders to death. But most of the kids at our school think she's
some kind of superhero.

Me, I think she's just like how God would be if He were
a lady. And who knows? Maybe She *is*. I just hope that
when I go to heaven, God is as nice as Principal Obermeyer about listening to all your mistakes. And not thinking you're so terrible after all. Just kind of mixed up. And
maybe She'll let you wear Her old sweatshirt, wrap you up
in a big quilt, and serve you hot cocoa.

Sometimes I go and talk to Principal after school about
stuff—about my sister, my dad, and missing Grandpa. It
was Principal's idea to put a special brass plaque by the
flagpole, where I spilled Grandpa's ashes. And have a special dedication ceremony for him. So the flagpole will be a
place to always remember him. Instead of a place where I
thought I lost him.

I reached under my pillow and grabbed my latest bag of
bridge mix and stuck it in my good dress-up purse. To
share with Nit after the ceremony. I get bridge mix almost
every day now under my pillow. Mom found out about
that, too, but doesn't seem to mind too much. She says
Maxey is working some things out right now, just like I am.

But Mom says not to get too used to it. Regular bossy
Maxey will be back soon.

I'm counting on it. And this time, I'll be ready.

ABOUT THE AUTHOR

MARY HERSHEY was raised by a pack of comedians disguised as actual family members, whom she adores. She says being a little sister is a good gig if you can get it, and being a big sister is harder than it looks. Mary Hershey has a master's degree in counseling and guidance and loves to swim and practice Yoga for Very Stiff People. She works full-time as an administrator for the Department of Veterans Affairs in Santa Barbara, California, where she lives with her partner and two rapscallion cats. This is her first novel.